NOBU FUKUI
252 Hambletonian RD,
Chester, NY 10918
917-565-3557
nobufk@Gmail.com

THE TAMA RIVER

NOBU FUKUI

ISBN-10: 069228432X
ISBN-13: 978-0692284322
TTR Publishing, New York, NY
Library of Congress Control Number: 2014915735

Nobu Fukui is an artist who lives and works in New York City.

Book Design: Daniel Ferris LLC, New York, NY

Cover Art: Nobu Fukui

TO KWISOON

THE VILLAGE   7

SUMO WRESTLING MATCH   15

THE ACCIDENT   23

PICTURE-BOOK WITHOUT PICTURES   33

THE SOUND OF LIFE   41

RAINING MOON   49

RAINBOW   61

FOUR-LEAF CLOVER   71

SUN PRINCES   79

THE KISS   87

DEATH   97

ZEN TEMPLE   107

BIRTHDAY   117

FORTUNE TELLER   125

BIGGEST FOOL ON EARTH   135

KAMIKAZE SENSEI   145

THE CATCHER'S MITT   155

CRAWFISH   165

GOODBYE   177

JEAN MARTINON   187

IN THE MUSEUM   201

EPILOGUE   209

THE VILLAGE

Minemachi Elementary School was located right by the Tama River on the outskirts of Tokyo. The building was an L-shaped, two story high wooden structure. It was built in 1947, two years after World War II ended. There were two square stone posts serving as the main gate leading to the school yard. The entire school property was enclosed by a wire fence with two other smaller gates. Five cherry trees were planted alongside the dike of the Tama River. The school year starts in April in Japan when the cherry blossoms are in full bloom.

It was 1954; I was eleven years old and going into sixth grade. The new school year didn't excite me at all; rather it was depressing. It was depressing to see those same old faces. In those days, at Minemachi

Elementary School, once you were placed in a class in the first grade, your placement carried all through six years until you graduated. There were no changes of classmates, even the teacher remained the same. By the time I was in the fourth grade, I was branded a bully. I didn't have even a single friend, and no one liked me. I thought it wasn't fair because I never badgered or intimidated anyone without a reason. I only went after those kids who called me *Balloon*. I was tall, the tallest in the class and very fat with a big round face. I didn't mind being called fat or even *Fatso* so much because it was a fact. But *Balloon*, I couldn't take because there's nothing inside a balloon except air. I thought it was the ultimate insult to be called *Balloon*. There was another reason why I was so wary of the new school year. The teacher who had taught our class from the first grade until the fifth grade had left the school and a new teacher had been assigned to our class. The new teacher's name was Mr. Yoshida, but kids called him 'Kamikaze Sensei' as he was known to exercise a military type discipline. He had been a physical education teacher until last year, but he had never had his own class before. Kids were terrified of Mr. Yoshida. If he saw a group of children running around in the hallway, he would line them up and slap their faces, but nobody dared to complain. In those days in Japan, teachers had absolute authority.

There were three new kids in the class, two boys and a girl. They were introduced to the class on the first day of school. The first boy's name was Toshio, and he was a good looking muscular kid with curly hair. The second one was a dirty looking skinny boy, and his name was Saburo.

"Chosenjin," as soon as the boy was introduced, some kid whispered, but it was loud enough for the entire class to hear.

"Who said that?" Mr. Yoshida asked sharply. The room fell silent.

"Who is it, raise your hand!" The vein was showing on his face. Mr. Yoshida was yelling now.

"It was Kenji." A boy named Yousuke pointed his finger at the boy sitting next to him.

"Kenji, stand up!" Walking down the aisle to the boy, Mr. Yoshida said, "was it you?"

Kenji nodded, but did not stand up. Mr. Yoshida grabbed Kenji's left earlobe and made him stand up, and dragged him down to the front of the classroom, and slapped his face so hard that he fell on the floor. Then he kicked Kenji's buttocks.

"Listen, everyone." Mr. Yoshida turned to the class. "Saburo is a Korean, but he was born in Japan, and he speaks Japanese just like you do. There is absolutely no difference between you and Saburo. If you ever call him Chosenjin, you will be punished."

During World War II, many Koreans were conscripted by the Japanese government, and over six hundred thousand of them were brought to mainland Japan for forced labor. Most of them went home after the war, but some remained in Japan. They were denied Japanese citizenship, even their children, who were born in Japan, could not attain citizenship.

By Japanese law, compulsory education applied to only those children whose parents, at least one of them, were Japanese citizens. Koreans were not required to send their children to school, and the schools were not obligated to accept them. Those who were lucky enough to be accepted by a school were allowed to stay but were at the mercy of the teachers and the principal. If they did not like the child, they were allowed to kick him or her out anytime without any explanation. Chosenjin means Korean, but the word was applied derogatorily to those Koreans in Japan.

"Go back to your desk." Kenji was still down on the floor crying. Mr. Yoshida grabbed Kenji's arm and made him stand up.

"Yousuke, stand up!" Mr. Yoshida called out. "I don't like what you did; I didn't ask anybody to point out who said it, did I?"

"No, sir," Yousuke stood up and answered, looking down but pursing his lips in protest.

While all this was going on, the three new students were kept standing in the corner; all had frightened looks on their faces. The girl who was short and skinny, and rather frail looking, looked especially frightened and had tears in her eyes. Finally Mr. Yoshida went to the girl and gently put his hand on her shoulder and introduced her to the class. Her name was Harumi. She had long shiny beautiful black hair. The classroom was crowded with forty children and Mr. Yoshida had to find desks for the new kids. Saburo was told to sit next to me.

The classes were boring; the entire school was boring. The reading materials we were given, I thought, were silly. Arithmetic was an uninteresting laborious brain exercise. I was studying my sister's math book at home, and found algebra fascinating. Using X's and Y's, problems were solved like magic. I brought some books from home, and during the class, I put one on my lap and read. I started to do this when I was in fourth grade, and our middle-aged female teacher tried to stop me, but I never listened and even argued about it, and eventually she gave up. Somehow, Mr. Yoshida left me alone. I thought he didn't notice it. I was reading Les Miserables by Victor Hugo and *No Longer Human* by Osamu Dazai, two totally different types of literature simultaneously. The story of *Les Miserables* was fascinating, but more and more I was drawn to the writings of Osamu Dazai who made several suicide attempts unsuccessfully before finally succeeding at the age of thirty eight. All his writings were generated by his profound pessimism. My father, who was a failed writer himself, later found out I was reading Dazai and took all his books and hid them from me. He thought Dazai was a bad influence.

I did homework and my test scores were good, so neither my teacher nor my parents had any complaint as far as my academics were concerned.

The boy who sat next to me, Saburo, was constantly in trouble from the beginning. Often he was late to school, he did not do his homework, and he didn't have proper notebooks, and I noticed that he didn't even have a pencil. Kamikaze Sensei was brutal. He made Saburo stand up all morning until lunch break for not bringing his homework for the third straight day. He slapped his face for not answering his questions. When I noticed that he didn't have a pencil, I put one on his desk. He took it without saying anything. I liked that. I didn't want him to thank me. I didn't want anyone to know about it either. The following day, I gave him two brand new notebooks. This time, Saburo looked at me puzzled, and tried to say something.

"Take them, and don't say anything," I whispered and made an angry face.

We were not wealthy; rather we were a struggling to survive, lower middle class family with five children. To my father, the most important thing was the education of his children. He made sure we had everything we needed in school. We had a stack of notebooks and boxes of new pencils always on the bookshelf. He had quite a collection of books also; there was almost a complete collection of major Japanese literature published prior to the war and lots of European literature. Sometimes teachers came to our house to borrow books from my father. Because of the war, some books were still hard to find.

I had two older sisters in middle school and two younger brothers in the same elementary school; we were all two years apart in age. All of us became ardent readers. There were absolutely no toys in the house, but we had an abundance of books for all levels. As soon as we learned to read, each of us started to pick up books from the bookshelves randomly, and read with our father's encouragement and guidance.

We had classes on Saturdays too, though the school ended at twelve noon. One Saturday afternoon, I was walking out of the school yard through the main gate, and I remembered that I had left the drawing I did in the art class that day on my desk. I really liked what I made, and I wanted to show it to my father. So I went back to the classroom. In the corner of the classroom, I found Saburo sitting on the floor crying.

"What happened?" I asked. He didn't say anything; he didn't even look at me. "What happened?" I yelled. He raised his face and looked at me, but he had a frightened look.

"Tell me what happened, don't be afraid," I said calmly. He was still hesitating.

"Kenji and two other kids..." Saburo finally opened his mouth and muttered.

"What did they do to you?" Saburo didn't answer and I repeated. "Tell me, what did they do to you?" Still silent, I was losing my temper and kicked the floor and asked again. You have to tell me what happened."

"They are waiting for me." He started to cry again.

"Where?" I said impatiently. "Stop crying, and tell me where they are!"

"At the rear gate."

"Okay, let's go!" I grabbed his arm, made him stand up, and started to head out. Saburo was still standing looking lost. I had to go to him and put my hand on his back, and I pushed him.

I saw three kids standing behind the wire fence. This small gate was opened only in the morning and at dismissal time. It was closed while classes were in session. Apparently, one of the kids saw me and said something to the others, and started to walk away, but two of the boys stopped him. Now they were blocking the gate and looking straight at me.

"Wait here," I told Saburo and went running up to the kids, and without a word I punched the kid who was standing in the center in the stomach. The kid was Kenji, and he bent over and fell on the ground. The kid on the right tried to punch me in the face, but I kicked his groin and his fist swung in the air. The third kid started to run, and the other kid stood up and ran also, Kenji followed.

"Stinking Chosenjin and overblown *Balloon*, good match!" they yelled as they were running away. "Stinking Chosenjin and overblown *Balloon!*"

I didn't go after them, but I swore to myself that I would get them next week for what they said.

"Were they bothering you every day?" Saburo was looking miserable and hopeless. For a moment, I hated him for that.

"Not every day," Saburo mumbled. "This is the second time; the first day of school they took my backpack and took everything inside except the textbooks."

That was the reason he didn't have anything, not even a pencil. He said that his parents were upset over his loosing things, and they wouldn't buy him any replacements because they did not have money.

"All right, I'll walk you home." I started to walk, but Saburo was still standing still.

"It's okay; you don't want to come to where I live," said Saburo still looking down.

"Let's go!" I started to walk, and Saburo reluctantly followed.

We walked about ten blocks along the dike of the Tama River, and I was beginning to understand why Saburo didn't want me to come with him. We were coming into the village. It was called *Chosenjin Buraku* which means Korean Village. We were all told by our parents never to go near the village. We were warned that it wasn't a safe place; we could be robbed and even killed if we stepped into the village. It would be a lie if I said that I wasn't afraid. I was a little afraid, but my curiosity was stronger than my fear. Besides, if Saburo wasn't afraid, why should I be afraid? It did not make any sense, so I went on. Saburo and I were both silent. There were rows and rows of makeshift houses made of plywood, old doors, some blankets and tin roofs, and there was a strong odor of rotten food.

"My house is down there, please go home." Saburo stopped and looked at me. "No, I want to see you to your house."

"No you don't!" For the first time Saburo looked alert and spoke firmly. He even seemed a little angry. I was taken aback, so I turned around and left.

'Some dog houses are built better than those,' I was thinking. 'Why, why do they have to live like that?' Our family lived in a one story, two family ranch style house with three small tatami rooms plus a kitchen and bath with an *Ofuro*; which is a traditional oval shaped deep wooden bathtub with a wood-burning cast iron boiler attached. There was no running water, but we had a hand pumped well in the kitchen and bathroom area. I had my own little desk and chair made of rattan palm and thin plywood in the two tatami room adjacent to the entryway. There was even a small garden at the front of our house. The garden was very important to my mother. She planted all sorts of vegetables and flowers, and spent hours every day taking care of them. The house was too small for a family of seven, yet, it was heaven compared to the houses I saw in the village. I didn't know why, but I was angry. I was so angry that my eyes were swelling up.

"Where have you been?" my mother asked me as soon as I came into the house. "I was worried about you."

"I took my friend home to the village," I said in a challenging voice.

"You mean Korean Village? Oh dear, I told you...."

"I am going to do it every day from now on!" I interrupted my mother. I didn't want to hear it.

Sumo Wrestling Match

Since that incident, I walked Saburo to the village after school every day. Saburo didn't ask me to, and I didn't say anything, but it just became a kind of routine. We didn't talk much, just quietly walked down to the edge of the village and then I turned around and went home.

We never saw Kenji's gang again, probably because I punished them again the following week, going after them one by one, and told each of them I would come after him whenever he bothered Saburo. One of the three, a kid named Kazuo put up some fight, and I hit him in the face pretty hard. It was before the morning assembly in the schoolyard, and by the time we settled in the classroom, his face was swollen and he had a black eye.

"Kazuo, what happened?" Mr. Yoshida quickly noticed it.

"Nobuo hit me for no reason," Kazuo complained. Now, I was the focal point of the entire class.

"Stand up, when you speak to me!" said Mr. Yoshida who then turned to me. "Nobuo, why did you hit Kazuo?"

"He, Kenji and Takeshi were ambushing Saburo," I stood up and declared. "When I tried to stop them, they called Saburo stinking *Chosenjin*, and called me overblown *Balloon*." I was not completely truthful but,"hit him for no reason"? I was mad.

"Is that true, Saburo? Saburo nodded.

"Nobuo, if you observe something like that, don't get into fight, just report it to me and let me handle it."

"I didn't want to bother you, sir," I answered.

"It's better to bother me than your resorting to violence."

'What a hypocrite!' I thought, wanting to spit in his face. 'He slaps kids left and right, and then tells me I cannot fight for cause?'

"Kenji and Takeshi, stand up!" Mr. Yoshida called out. "All four of you, go to the back and stand there until the first period is over."

I really didn't think I deserved to be punished equally with those three, but it wasn't too bad. That was that in the classroom. But late in the afternoon after school, Kazuo's mother visited my mother with reluctant Kazuo in tow. She was steaming mad.

"Please look at what your son did to my son!" I heard Kazuo's mother yelling, apparently showing Kazuo's face to my mother. I was in the back room listening. "I understand my son, Kazuo called your son 'Fatso" and your son was upset. He was wrong to call your son 'Fatso', but he used such excessive violence. This is absolutely not acceptable."

"I am very sorry." This was not the first time. Over the past few years, several parents had come to my mother and had complained about me. They all claimed that their children were innocent and just victims of my violence. Nobody wanted to hear my side of the story, not even my own mother.

"Nobuo, come here!" my mother called. I was kind of ready for this, and I was very wary. When his mother saw Kazuo's face, I knew she would come and complain. It was my mistake; I shouldn't have hit his face. "Apologize to Kazuo at once!" my mother demanded.

"It was a fair fight, Kazuo attacked me too," I said. "Hey, Kazuo, tell them the truth!" Kazuo was trying to hide behind his mother. "Next time, I won't punch you in the face; I will kick your ass!"

"Did you hear what he said?" Kazuo's mother said to my mother. She was becoming hysterical. "Your son will wind up in jail someday, you know. Yes, that's where he belongs, jail. I must talk to Mr. Yoshida."

She grabbed Kazuo's arm and turned around and left.

"I am sorry; I will talk to my son," speaking to their backs, my mother was almost in tears.

"What is wrong with you!?" My mother couldn't stand up. "How many times have I told you not to hit anyone? If Mr. Yoshida hears about this, he will send you to a reform school."

"No, he won't," I was laughing. "He knows all about it already; it was settled in school. No big deal."

"Why are you so mischievous? You make me worry and make me physically sick." She tried to grab my arm, but I shook it off. "Because of you, I never have peace of mind."

"Here we go again." I was getting upset. "Now you're going to tell me I have been a bad boy since I was born, no, even before I was born."

According to my mother, I was so comfortable in her tummy that I refused to come out for too long. She told me that she had such a hard labor, and I almost killed her. She had had a natural childbirth, and I was the biggest child ever born in the history of the hospital. I weighed ten pounds and three ounces. She was four foot eight inches high, a petite woman. But was it my fault? She made me believe that it was. I had been a bad boy to my mother since I was born.

I loved my mother though. I loved her more than anything in the world.

She was an absolute idol to me. She was a great cook, she played every traditional Japanese instrument, and especially she played thirteen-stringed *Koto* so beautifully that every time she played, neighbors would come to the front yard to listen. Her voice had incredible range. She sang traditional Japanese songs with the Shamisen, which is a three-stringed musical instrument that looks a bit like a banjo, and she sang American and European folk songs in English. She loved to listen to classical music; Mozart was her favorite composer, and his Clarinet Concerto was her favorite music. She was an excellent calligrapher, professional level. She studied at the Friends School, a Quaker-run girls' school in Tokyo, and was fluent in English. Sometimes, she would recite her favorite scenes from Shakespeare's plays in English. She was an artist too; she made drawings and transformed them into incredibly beautiful silk embroidery using a traditional Japanese technique. I was constantly awed by whatever she did. I worshiped her.

I loved to be touched by my mother's soft hands. How I wished to be embraced by her! It never happened. It wasn't that she was not affectionate; in fact she was very affectionate. She was constantly holding my youngest brother, Tomo. Tomo was seven years old, but she still sometimes held him in her arms on the futon until he fell asleep. The only time she touched me was when I was sick. I lay on a futon mattress with a high fever, and she came to my side and sat. She put her hand on my forehead. It made me feel very peaceful, and the pain, the fever and even my weight just dissolved. I felt as if my whole body were lifted in the air. Usually she stayed with me until I fell asleep.

I didn't know how to express my love for my mother either. The more I longed for her love, the more rebellious I became. I nagged her constantly, never said anything nice to her, and never listened to her. I did the exact opposite of what she wanted me to do. My mother became more and more distant from me as a result.

I started to pay a little attention to Saburo during class. I noticed that he didn't have many problems with reading and writing, but it seemed that he had some difficulty understanding math. There was math homework one day, and I suggested that we stay in the classroom after school and do homework together. Saburo loved the idea. He said that once he got home, he had to take care of his baby sister, and besides, there was no desk to do homework on. We spent about half an hour together and the homework was done. Actually, Saburo was very quick to learn. So, doing homework together after school became an addition to our routine.

The teacher of the class next to ours was absent one day. The principal of the school taught the class for half day, and Mr. Yoshida was put in charge of the two classes in the afternoon. There were no substitute teachers in the school at that time.

It was a warm sunny day, and the petals had been falling steadily but cherry blossoms were still in bloom. Mr. Yoshida took more than eighty children to the schoolyard. Somehow, he came up with the idea of a Sumo wrestling tournament for the boys. He took us to the corner of the schoolyard under the cherry trees. There was a large sandbox carved in the ground. Using his right foot, Mr. Yoshida drew a round ring in the sand. Then he made the forty five boys line up, from the shortest one to the tallest, and declared that the last boy standing would be the champion. The tallest boy would challenge the shortest boy to begin, and the winner of that match would face the next boy on the opposite side of the line. The girls were seated around the ring to watch. The boys were told to take their shirts and shoes off before getting into the ring for a match.

I was the tallest of all. I took my shirt off and hung it on the fence, and then I took my sneakers off and went into the ring. I started the match with the smallest boy.

I quickly put my arms around the boy's waist and grabbed his belt with two hands and carried him out of the ring. It was easy. I beat over ten boys in a similar manner. Then I faced Kazuo, the boy I punched on the face, and whose mother went to complain to Mr. Yoshida. I hadn't heard about the incident ever since, so I assumed that Mr. Yoshida had explained to her what had really happened. I somehow believed in Mr. Yoshida's fairness.

Mr. Yoshida gave the signal and we started. Kazuo was rather a smart wrestler and a courageous one as well. He immediately jumped sideways and escaped my hold. I guess he had figured out if he got caught by me, he would have no chance. As he was jumping sideways, he tried to kick my left leg. His foot scratched my leg, and for a moment I lost my balance. Kazuo took the opportunity, and he banged his body into the side of my body. I barely survived this blow, but somehow I managed to get hold of his belt and I threw him into the sand really hard. It was a wake up call for me. It shook me up, and made me think that I should be more alert and serious about my opponents. But this match with Kazuo had an unexpected effect on the waiting boys. It inflicted some fear in them. The next one looked obviously afraid of me. I put my right arm under his left arm and flew him into the sand. The following boys behaved similarly; they seemed to be afraid to attack and instead were looking for an easy and painless defeat. I decided to show no mercy, and I buried every one of them in the sand.

The only exception was Saburo. When he faced me, waiting for Mr. Yoshida's signal, I saw fire in his eyes. I could see he was determined to put up a good fight. He was skinny and rather tall. I thought the match would be over quickly if I could catch him. I decided to wait for his move. He kept his head down and dashed at me, and attacked my right leg. He grabbed my leg with two hands and tried to lift it off the ground, and he was successful for a few moments. I was standing with one leg and Saburo was pushing me with all his might. I danced back a few steps, and I heard some kids gasp. But I held on and got my leg free of his grasp. Then, I hooked my left leg to his right leg, and bent forward to put my weight over his body

He collapsed under me in the sand.

None of the kids who followed Saburo gave me much trouble. The last one was a muscular new kid, Toshio. Toshio was a happy kid. He was bright and funny, and in such a short while, he had become very popular, in fact, he was the most popular kid in the class. Sometimes he even made Kamikaze Sensei laugh.

I was getting very tired and thirsty. I wasn't sure if I had enough energy to fight this boy. I told Mr. Yoshida that I was thirsty and wanted some water. He obliged and sent two girls to fetch a glass of water for me. I went out of the circle and sat on the wooden boundary of the sand box and waited. Toshio was standing on the opposite side of me and smiling. I knew I had to come up with some strategy to beat him. I thought he would probably overpower me if I went directly against him. Toshio was still smiling talking to some kids. It seemed as though he was always smiling. 'How can he be so happy all the time?' I wondered. I didn't like it. I couldn't stand seeing his smile, and felt like slapping his face to stop his smile, and that gave me an idea.

The two girls came back with a glass of water. I emptied the glass with one gulp. I stood up and stepped into the ring. At the same time Toshio stepped into the ring as well, still smiling. I thought he was showing off his confidence.

"Deflate that dirty balloon." I couldn't tell who, but someone yelled, and some kids burst into laughter.

Both of us crouched, and instantly Mr. Yoshida gave the start signal. Toshio dashed toward me with full force expecting me to do the same, but I stepped slightly to his left and swung my right hand over his face. I felt a sharp pain on my palm. The blow made Toshio stumble badly to his right, and without missing a beat, I threw my whole body onto him. Toshio fell backward in the sand with me on top of him. It was so quick; everyone around the ring seemed to be stunned and speechless including Mr. Yoshida. I stood up and gave my hand to help Toshio up.

"True champion!" declared Mr. Yoshida as he lifted my right arm high.

"It wasn't fair!" Some kids yelled out. "He hit Toshio!"

"Yeah, Nobuo wasn't fair!" A lot of kids were muttering.

"Slapping is one of the recognized skills in Sumo," Mr. Yoshida announced. "Nobuo won fair and square."

I looked at Toshio; he was covering his left ear with his hand. His face showed agonizing pain. I must have hit his ear. I wasn't happy though, I was just exhausted and feeling lonely. I didn't know why, but I wanted to cry. Brushing off the sand from my body and my pants, I went to the fence and retrieved my shirt and put it on. I was sweating but felt chilly even after I had put on my shirt.

We all headed back to the classroom. The entire crowd walked slowly with an awkward silence. I didn't realize Saburo was walking next to me. When I noticed, he looked at me with a gentle smile. I tried to smile back, but my eyes started to swell, and I had to turn around and look up.

Mr. Yoshida told us that we were free to do anything until dismissal as long as we were quiet at our desks. I didn't feel like doing anything, so I put my arms on the desk and buried my face pretending to be asleep. I wanted to get out of the classroom as soon as possible.

Finally, the bell rang. I picked up my backpack and ran out of the classroom. I ran across the yard, and through the side gate and I headed to the dike of the river. I ran up the slope and when I reached the top of the dike I took a deep breath.

I threw my backpack to the bottom of the slope, and I lay my body flat on the grass and pushed the ground with my right arm. I closed my eyes and my body was rolling down the slope. Before I knew I was at the bottom. It was too quick. I went up the slope and rolled again. This time I kept my eyes open. I saw blue sky rolling down with me, but it stopped too soon. I went up the slope again, as I was rolling down, I felt that the sky and my body became one, and when I reached the bottom, I closed my eyes. My body enveloped by the clear blue sky kept rolling, rolling, and rolling down forever.

I didn't know how long I stayed there. I heard some footsteps in the distance and I opened my eyes. I looked around and found Saburo walking down the slope slowly. He came to where I was lying and sat down without a word. I sat up next to him and watched the river and beyond. The river was high with water and flowing rapidly. On the other side of the river, I saw neatly lined up red roofs and a number of chimneys of different heights. But somehow everything looked so unreal.

THE ACCIDENT

When I woke up, I was all wrapped up with bandages in a hospital bed. I hardly remembered anything. The first person I recognized was my father. He was smiling, but with teary eyes.

"How do you feel?" he asked, bending over my face. I couldn't say anything. I couldn't open my mouth nor could I make any sound. My body was totally numb; I didn't even have any pain.

"Oh, you are back, conscious now." A nurse came in. "Very good, very good!"

I couldn't move my head, but I moved my eyes around and looked for my mother. She wasn't there.

No one told me the whole story, but I pieced together what had happened after listening to my father and the nurse. I had an accident. I was hit by a three wheel pickup truck on the way from school. In those days in Tokyo, especially in suburban Tokyo, the streets were narrow and there were no sidewalks. The three wheel pickup truck was the most popular commercial vehicle in the city, and there were so many of them around. I was walking down the street near our home. The driver of the three wheel truck lost control and hit me from behind. I banged my head on the stone wall of a house, my left arm was broken, and my right leg was dislocated at the knee. I was bruised all over my body. The doctors worried that I must have fractured some ribs, but that turned out negative.

"You were lucky; there was no damage to your scull or brain," the nurse told me. "The cushion on your body must have protected your bones a little too." She was laughing.

"You mean my being fat prevented more damage to my bones?" I couldn't believe what she was saying. I wasn't sure about brain damage either. I didn't remember what street I was walking on when I was hit. I couldn't remember the day of the week or the month.

I had no recollection of what I had done in school or what book I had been reading that day. I was convinced that my brain was damaged somehow, and nobody even knew about it.

My mother came to see me the next day. She said she was busy with something, but I wasn't even listening. After two days of lying still, I was able to sit up on the bed.

"Young bodies recover quickly," the doctor was saying. "You will be able to go home soon."

On the day I was discharged, my father came to pick me up. He gave me a piggyback from the hospital to our home, about twenty blocks. He was telling me some childish story all the way home, but I didn't mind, I rather enjoyed it. This was a rare occasion where my father showed affection toward any of his children. Unlike my mother, he was not affectionate at all. He was a quiet, detached man. He was always reading or writing something. My sisters complained often that he hardly talked to them.

I came home with plaster casts on my left arm and my right leg, and a bandage on my bald head. I was told that they had shaved my head for the doctor to examine the wound. My father took me to the hospital on his back a few more times. Soon, I was able to walk with a crutch. It was so boring staying home doing nothing. Strangely ,I missed school, the school I hated so much. There was nothing specific that I missed. I guess I just missed the routine. I nagged my father to carry me to school. He told me that I had to wait for the plaster cast to be removed from my leg.

On the first day of returning to school, my mother came with me carrying my backpack. I was told to use a crutch although I had no problem walking without it. I had a bandage on my head, and my left arm was still in the cast supported by the wide white cloth which was hung from my neck.

All the way to school, my mother was lecturing me. I must be nice to everyone; I should listen to teachers, that kind of stuff. When I walked into the classroom, the class was already in session. Mr. Yoshida greeted my mother at the door, and they talked outside for a few minutes. I took my backpack from my mother's hand, and hung it over my right shoulder. I walked slowly to my desk in the back with the crutch under my right arm.

"Patched up *Balloon*," somebody whispered and there was some laughter.

Saburo stood up, and pulled the chair out for me. I sat down and managed to smile at him. I was already regretting my decision to come to school.

It was the same old boring stuff. I tried to read one of the books I had brought from home, but I couldn't hold it open on my lap with one hand, so I gave up. Time passed irritatingly slowly.

Lunch time was always chaotic. There was no such thing as a dining hall or cafeteria. Students took turns each day. Two kids would go to the kitchen and roll a cart full of trays down the hallway to the classroom. Each child was expected to go to the front of the classroom and fetch his or her own tray. Saburo took two trips and brought me my tray without a word. I was not used to this kind of kindness or friendship from my peers. I felt awkward, even a little embarrassed and I couldn't thank him.

On the lunch tray, there was a peanut butter sandwich; two pieces of bread bound together with thinly spread peanut butter, a cup of milk which was made from powdered milk, and some fruit; a little apple or a tangerine. The sandwich was okay, edible, but the milk tasted horrible. Once, instead of an apple or orange, there was a banana on the tray. Bananas were mostly imported from Hawaii or Taiwan and were very expensive those days. Most of the kids had never eaten bananas before.

"Banana day!" The kids who went to get the cart for the class screamed when they saw bananas on the lunch trays. "Banana day!" The chorus echoed throughout the school building. Kids went crazy.

Mr. Yoshida once explained that the food for lunch was being supplied by American aid, but this would soon change because the Peace Treaty had come into force and Japan had become an independent country two years ago. He thought that we would be served Japanese food for lunch soon.

After finishing lunch, kids took the trays back to the cart, and went outside. I was left alone. I put a book on the desk to read, but then I realized there was another kid sitting in the middle of the classroom. It was a girl. It took a little while to figure out who she was. It was Harumi, the new girl. Harumi was reading a book also, and I became a little curious. After reading several pages, I stood up and grabbed the crutch and went behind her and peeked. It was one of the books called *Bunkobon*, publishers' series books. I didn't like those because they were small paperbacks and the font was so small. They were not easy to read.

"This is Tolstoy," Harumi looked up and showed me the cover. "*Anna Karenina*." I hadn't read any of his books, but I had a vague idea who Tolstoy was. Two books of his were sitting on my father's bookshelf. I was sure one of them was titled *Anna Karenina*.

"Why are you staying in the classroom?" I asked. "Don't you go and play outside?" It was the rule that we had to be out in the schoolyard after we finished lunch.

26

"I can't," Harumi looked down and said. "I cannot do any physical activities, my doctor told me. What have you been reading?" Turning around and looking at me, Harumi changed the subject.

"How do you know I have been reading a book?" I was shocked by her question.

"Everybody knows," Harumi laughed. "You put the book on your lap and read all the time; I bet the teacher knows too."

I couldn't believe it. I thought that the only one who knew about it was Saburo. Did he tell everybody? No way would he do that.

"What are you reading now?" Harumi asked again.

"*Les Miserables*," I mumbled. I was a slow reader, and still hadn't finished the book, besides; I was reading short stories by Ryunosuke Akutagawa at the same time.

"That's funny, you know, Tolstoy was kind of influenced by Victor Hugo." Harumi's eyes lit up. "Tolstoy loved *Les Miserables*."

"How come you know so much about literature?" I didn't even know they were from the same period.

"I love books. That's why. You love books too, I know," Harumi said. "Why don't you sit down?"

I sat on the chair across the aisle from her.

"Who is your favorite author?" she asked. I felt I was being tested.

"I like Osamu Dazai, but my father took all his books away from me and hid them," I said. "He thinks Dazai is a bad influence. I don't see why though."

"Oh no, Osamu Dazai. I don't like him at all!" Harumi exclaimed. "I hate his writing. It makes you feel like life is not worth living; we should all die."

"No it doesn't," I had to protest. "His stories are pessimistic, but beautiful."

"I have no time for pessimism," Harumi said firmly. "I want to enjoy living."

Kids were coming back into the classroom. I stood up and went back to my desk.

After the bell, Saburo and I remained at our desks and waited for all the other kids to leave. We had some homework to do.

"What are you doing?" Harumi came over and asked me.

"What do you mean?" I pretended I didn't know what she was talking about.

"You and Saburo always stay in the classroom after everyone else is gone." Harumi was looking at my eyes. "What are you doing?"

"Have you been spying on us?" I said. "You are so nosey."

"No, I was just curious." Harumi was laughing.

"We are doing homework together," Saburo answered.

"That's cool, can I join you guys?" Harumi was tiptoeing anxiously. Saburo and I looked at each other. Saburo nodded.

"All right," I said.

"This is so, so cool" She took her backpack down from her shoulder, and sat on the chair in front of me.

Today's homework was simple. We must remember how to write twenty-five new *Kanji*. *Kanji* means Chinese characters. We will have a test tomorrow. I hated *Kanji*, I had no problem reading them, but it was so hard to remember how to write them. Over 1800 Chinese characters were used in Japanese written language, and we were supposed to remember 881 of them before we were graduated from elementary school. What a daunting task!

I proposed that we practice writing them ourselves for a while, and then we would take turns and give mock tests to each other. I gave a test to Harumi and Saburo first. Saburo had six wrong, but Harumi had a perfect score. Since Harumi was perfect, we asked her to give us tests until we had perfect scores. At the first mock test Harumi gave us, I had eight wrong and Saburo had two wrong. At the next test Saburo was perfect. It took me four more tests to get it all right. Harumi and Saburo tried very hard to show me how to remember them, but still I had some trouble.

Saburo headed to the rear gate and went home by himself. I left my backpack under the desk since I knew I would have trouble carrying it back home. Harumi and I walked through the front gate and headed home.

"Are you all right?" Harumi asked me with worried look. "Can you really walk home?"

"I walked to school this morning," I said. I was holding the crutch under my right arm, but I wasn't really leaning on it. "Look, I could walk without this." I lifted the crutch off the ground and swung it in the air.

"Please don't!" Harumi said. We walked silently for a while.

"What do you do on Sundays usually?" Harumi stopped at the corner and asked.

It turned out that Harumi's house was just three blocks away from my house. Harumi said that she had to turn at the corner.

"Before the accident, I went to the Tama River and did drawings every Sunday," I answered.

"Wow, really? That sounds fantastic!" Harumi looked at me with twinkling eyes. "Do you think you could do that this Sunday?"

"Sure!" I said, although I wasn't sure if I could do it with my left arm in a plaster cast and strapped from my neck.

"Can I come with you?" Harumi was still watching my face. "I will help you carry your stuff, so please?"

"Yeah, that will be great!" I felt Harumi's excitement, which made me excited.

"What time do you want to go?" Harumi asked, and I said it should be after lunch. We agreed that we would meet on the corner at one o'clock on Sunday.

"It's a promise." With her both hands, Harumi touched my right hand which was holding the crutch; I pulled my hand away in reaction. She held it tight for a second and let go.

I watched her hopping down the street until she disappeared.

The next morning, my mother took me to the hospital. The doctor took the bandage off my head and examined the wound carefully, and then took the stitches out. I didn't need the bandage any more. Then he checked my left leg and said that I didn't have to use the crutch if I didn't want to.

"You cannot go to school like that," as we were coming out of the hospital, looking at my head, my mother said. I touched the scar on my head with my fingers. She took me to a clothing store and bought me a blue baseball cap, and told me to wear it until my hair grew back.

When I walked into the classroom, kids were eating lunch. Harumi gave me a big smile, and it lifted my spirits. Since I knew that I should not wear a cap in the classroom, I went to Mr. Yoshida who was at the desk, and took my baseball cap off and showed him my scar.

"You may keep it on," Mr. Yoshida took a glance at my head and said. "You don't need a crutch?"

"No sir, the doctor told me not to run though," I said.

"You should remain in the classroom after lunch for a while," Mr. Yoshida said. "Don't go out."

I took a tray from the cart and went to my desk and sat down. All the while, Harumi was watching me.

All the kids were out in the schoolyard, and Harumi and I stood by the window looking outside. It was a beautiful day with not a speck of cloud in the sky.

"What a beautiful day!" Harumi said. It sounded as if she were reciting poetry. "I was born on a beautiful spring day like this, that's why my parents gave me the name *Harumi*."

Haru means spring in Japanese and *Mi* means beauty.

"I love my name, *Harumi*." Harumi looked at me with her twinkling eyes and said, "Your name Nobuo means extending man; who gave you the name?"

"My grandfather." The Chinese character used for Nobu has a meaning of extending and O means man. "I don't like my name," I said.

"Why? You will be a man, when you grow up, who extends your kindness, wisdom........"

"Stop it!" I yelled. "Don't make a fun of me!"

"I am not," said Harumi and looked down. "I like your name." I looked at Harumi's face and saw a shadow of sadness passing. I felt a sudden pain in my heart.

"Thank you," I said and tried to smile unsuccessfully. "I like your name, *Harumi*, very much, it suits you well."

We stood there in silence for a while. I felt awkward and didn't know what to do. I hated myself.

"I am looking forward to going to the river with you this Sunday." Harumi rescued me with her smile.

"I am too!" I said excitedly. You know what? The doctor is going to take the plaster cast off my arm on Saturday, so I will have my left arm back!"

"That's great!"

PICTURE-BOOK WITHOUT PICTURES

I woke up early in the morning, and took out a drawing pad and a small case of an oil pastel set. I had breakfast, and there was nothing to do. Why didn't I decide to go in the morning? We could have spent the whole day at the river together? I was restless. I could not wait until one o'clock. Around eleven thirty, I asked my mother to make lunch for me.

"Why so early?" mother asked. I did tell her last night that I would go to the river after lunch today.

"I want to do a lot of drawing today," I said. "I couldn't go out for a long time because of the accident, you know."

I finished my lunch before noon. I couldn't stand it any longer, so I decided to leave the house. I tried to hold the drawing pad under my left arm, but it just slipped and I dropped it. I realized my left arm didn't have any strength. The doctor warned me, but I felt really weird. It did not take me long to get to the corner, and I waited. I didn't have a watch, so I had no idea how long I was standing there.

I recognized Harumi from the distance. She was approaching steadily, but I felt as if she was walking very slowly on purpose.

"Oh, you are here already," Harumi said looking surprised. "I thought I was too early, it's not one o'clock yet. Were you waiting long?"

"No, I just came," I lied.

Harumi was carrying a little red backpack on her back. We took the shortest road to the river. When we reached the dike, I just wanted to run up the slope. There were no steps to go up to the top at this spot. But as soon as I put my leg on the slope, I slipped on the grass and fell on my butt.

"Are you all right?" Harumi came and tried to help me up. She held my hand and tried to pull me, but I couldn't get up and struggled. After a few attempts, I managed to stand up. Harumi kept holding my hand, and did not let go even after I got up. Her hand was bony and cold and she was squeezing my hand so gently. We walked along the dike a while, and found narrow stone steps leading to the top.

How I loved the view from the top of the dike where the narrow path was stretching in both directions endlessly. I saw green grass spreading to the river, and then the strong water flow. Over the other side of the river you could see a bunch of tiny houses, a number of chimneys at different heights, and big steel towers with cables in between. On the far side of the river, you could see a bridge with the freight train running on it. You could turn around and look toward where you came from; you could see rows of small houses backed by gentle hills with lots and lots of different shades of green trees. I also loved to walk on the path on top of the dike which was about eight feet wide and twenty feet above the bank of the river.

I decided to draw the other side of the river where steel towers were standing. We went several steps down toward the river and sat down. I opened the drawing pad and put it on my lap, and started to draw with oil pastels. Harumi took the little red backpack off her shoulder and opened it.

"Can I read you a book, while you are drawing?" She took out a little paperback book and looked at me.

"Sure, but what book, Anna Karenina?" I thought the book could be a little too heavy to enjoy in this circumstance, and it was way too long.

"Of course not!" Harumi said. "*Anna Karenina*, you must read yourself."

"That's what I thought. What book is it then?" I stopped drawing and tried to look at the book.

"It's a Hans Christian Andersen book," said Harumi, opening the book.

"You mean *The Little Mermaid*, *The Emperor's New Clothes*, *The Ugly Duckling*....," I said contentiously. "That kind of kids' stuff?"

"No, no, no," Harumi protested. This is my favorite Andersen book called *A Picture-Book Without Pictures*."

"I never heard of it." I thought I knew most of his fairy tales.

"This is not exactly a kids' book, but don't forget, we are still kids, you know," said Harumi, looking up at my face with a smile.

"This poor young artist came to town and was living without any friend or acquaintance," Harumi explained. "One evening, the moon came to his window and promised him to tell what she had seen the past night. The moon came back to his window for thirty nights. So, there are thirty short stories in this book."

"That sounds very interesting." I became curious. "Please read it to me."

"*Strange it is*," Harumi started to read. "*that at those very times when I am conscious of the warmest and best feelings, my hands and tongue seem, as it were, tied, so that I can express nothing, nor give utterance to any of the thoughts that fill my breast. And yet I am a painter......*"

At once, I was drawn to the story. Harumi's clear and sweet voice sounded like music and carried me to another world.

First Evening

Last night - these are the Moon's own words - I sailed through the clear air of India. I mirrored myself in the Ganges. My beams struggled to force a way through the thick roof of the old plane-trees, close and compact like the shell upon the tortoise. From out the thicket stepped a Hindu maiden, slender as a gazelle, beautiful as Eve. There was something truly ethereal, yet at the same time of corporeal beauty, about the Indian girl. I could discern her thought beneath her delicate skin. The thorny tendrils of the Liana tore her sandals; but she stepped swiftly through them. The wild beasts that came up from the river, where they had been to quench their thirst, fled affrightedly away, for the maiden held a burning lamp in her hand. I could see the fresh blood in those delicate fingers, which were arched into a screen over the flame of the lamp. She drew near to the river, placed the lamp upon the waters, and the lamp sailed away with the stream. The air was agitated, and it seemed that it must put out the light; but still the flame burned on, and the maiden's dark and sparkling eyes followed it, with a soul-speaking glance from beneath the long silken lashes of her eyelids. Well she knew, that if the lamp burned so long as she could follow it with her eye, her lover would be alive; but if it went out, then he would be dead. And the lamp burned and flickered, and the maiden's heart burned and quivered. She knelt down and said a prayer. Beside her lay a deadly serpent in the grass; but she thought only of Brahma, and of her beloved. "He lives!" she cried exultingly; and echo resounded from the hills, "He Lives!"

"Fantastic story, I love it!" I screamed. "Will you read it again?"

Harumi started to read again, and when she reached the last sentence I joined her and screamed, "He lives!"

She cried exultingly; Harumi read on, *An echo resounded from the hills,*

"He lives!" Harumi and I together cried exultingly. "He lives!"

After reading several more stories from the book, Harumi took out a lacquered wooden container from the backpack.

"Would you like some plum?" She picked a piece of plum from the box with two fingers and tried to hand it to me.

"Sure, but...." I looked at my hands. My fingers were colored with oil pastels. I put down the drawing pad on the grass and tried to wipe them off on my pants.

"No, don't do that." She lifted the hand holding the plum, and said, "Open your mouth." Harumi put the piece in my mouth, but did not let it go right away. Her fingers touched my lips. I felt some strange sensation running through my body. She gave me a second piece in the same manner, but this time she did not let go of the plum until I closed my mouth. Her two fingers were between my lips for a few seconds, and all the while her sparkling eyes were examining my face.

"I have two rice crackers, you want some?" Harumi was looking in the backpack. "I have some *daifuku* too."

"*Daifuku!?*" I screamed. *Daifuku* is a Japanese soft rice cake stuffed with sweet red bean paste. It was my favorite. I loved sweet Japanese pastries, especially those made with red beans. "You are so well prepared!"

"Open your mouth," holding one *daifuku* on her palm Harumi ordered.

"No, I don't want to bite your fingers," I said.

"Ha ha ...," Harumi started to laugh with her mouth opened. Her voice echoed in my ears, so clear, so sweet. She put a piece of rice paper around the *daifuku* and handed to me.

I lay down on the grass, and looked at the sky. A big white island of cloud was floating in the blue, and moving ever so slowly. I was happy, I thought, for the first time in my life, I was happy. I closed my eyes. I felt my body was lifted in the air and floating, and moving with the cloud.

"Do you want some water?"

I opened my eyes. Harumi was over my face so close. I was a little frightened. I said yes, and tried to get up.

"Stay like that," said Harumi, and she put her hands on my shoulders and pushed me back on the grass. She took out a small canteen from her backpack and opened the cap. She took a sip and turned around, pressed her mouth gently on my lips and released the water a little at a time into my mouth. I was stunned and motionless. I saw this huge face hovering over me, and her hair was surrounding my entire head like a fence. I felt like I was a captive and forced to accept some liquid in my mouth. Harumi had her eyes shut while doing it. When it was done, she was smiling with sparkling eyes, and took a deep breath as if she has just accomplished something very important.

"Yikes! You spit in my mouth," I jumped up and yelled.

"Didn't you like it?" Harumi was still smiling. "It's supposed to taste really good, no?"

"No, it didn't taste good." I was shocked. That was the truth. I didn't remember any taste. It was just cool liquid flowing into my mouth.

"I am sorry." Her smile was gone, and Harumi was looking disappointed. "You are so unromantic."

"Unromantic? What's romantic?" I had no idea what she was talking about.

"You see, I read a story in a magazine, a man was injured and couldn't move and he was dying of thirst. His girlfriend gave him some water from her mouth, and he said, 'The most delicious drink I ever had!' Harumi was explaining where she got the idea. "I thought it was so nice and romantic. The man dies at the end though."

"That's a terrible story." I was not upset or anything, just really shocked, and I didn't like the story or what she did.

I finished one drawing, and I wanted to go near the river. Usually, I would lie on the grass and roll down the slope, but I was worried about my left arm, so I started to walk down slowly. Harumi came and held my hand.

We came to the bank and watched the river. The water was flowing fast, and it was mesmerizing.

"Will you draw a picture of me?" Harumi turned and looked at me, and said.

"I don't know," I said. "It's difficult to draw people, I don't like portraits, I can't do it." Mr. Okamoto, our art teacher, had been encouraging me to draw figures. He said that all great artists trained themselves by drawing figures.

"I don't want you to draw my portrait; I just want to be a part of your drawing." Harumi was tiptoeing. I could see that she was getting excited with her own idea.

"What about this?" Harumi went close to the water and sat on the rock. "You draw all those rocks, grasses, water, whatever and me as another object. I will be looking at the water, so you won't see my face."

A person as another object, that was an idea, I never thought of that. I couldn't draw figures because the concept of *figure* was tying up my brain. I had read and was told so many times that one could not be an artist if one could not draw figures.

"I like the idea," I called out to Harumi, and felt the blood running up to my head.

I moved around to find a perfect spot to do the drawing. Harumi was sitting still patiently. I found a small rock not too far from Harumi and sat on it, and started to draw. I worked on it for a while, but I realized that it wasn't working. I moved around again for a while, but came back to the rock I was sitting on before.

"Will you turn to your left so that I could see your face a little?" I asked Harumi.

She moved a little, and let her long black hair flow down on her breast from her right shoulder. She looked stunningly beautiful. Funny, I had not noticed how beautiful she was until then.

Everything surrounding us became still, except the water which was repeating the same soft melody endlessly. Harumi was motionless; she became a statue. I lost the sense of time completely. I didn't know how long I worked on the drawing. Suddenly I felt that the energy was draining out of my body.

"Come and see what I have done," I broke the silence.

"Wow, is it done!?" she stood up, turned around, and exclaimed.

"No, it's not done," I said, as she was running to my side. "But I could finish it at home."

"It's beautiful!" said Harumi looking at the drawing. "Can I have it?" She was already tiptoeing.

"It's not finished yet!" I said. "When it's done I will give it to you."

"Really? Thank you, thank you." Harumi held my arm so tight it was almost painful.

We saw a big golden sun just above the bridge far away. It was getting ready to set into the horizon. We headed to the dike. Both Harumi and I had some trouble climbing up the slope. I held Harumi's hand and pulled her up. When we finally reached the path, Harumi sat down looking exhausted.

"Are you all right?" I was worried.

"Will you give me piggyback?" Harumi looked up and asked.

I crouched, and Harumi leaned over my shoulder and wrapped her arms around my neck. I gave her the drawing pad and the little case of oil pastels to hold. I had no problem standing up, holding her legs with my arms. Harumi held the drawing pad and the little case in her hands pressing onto my chest. As I walked down the path with Harumi's cheek on my shoulder, feeling her breath on my neck, I felt like a real grownup man. I was so proud of myself, and I was happy beyond words.

THE SOUND OF LIFE

Harumi was waiting for me at the corner in the morning. We said 'Hi' and Harumi held my hand. Since she did it so naturally I could not resist, although I was feeling a little awkward.

"Tiny girl's holding a big *Balloon!*" Hearing the voice, I turned around. Four kids, who were not from our class, were walking past us, all laughing and as soon as I saw them they started to run, and yelled. "Did you get married last night?"

I tried to free my hand from Harumi's and wanted to run after them.

"No, Nobuo!" said Harumi, now holding my wrist with her both hands. "Do not pay attention to them. It doesn't matter what they say or think"

Her eyes were piercing my eyes. Still I tried to free myself.

"If you go after them, I'll never speak to you again, and I mean it!" Harumi said in such a harsh tone. I was taken aback. Her eyes were still piercing my eyes.

Without a word, I started to walk, and Harumi took her hands off my wrist, but quickly held my left hand tightly. We walked to school in silence, but tremendous anger was boiling in my stomach. 'I must remember those kids. I will get them someday.'

Every morning, all the students were gathered in the school yard for assembly. Children were divided by each class, lined up from the first graders on the right side to sixth graders on the far left, also within each grade, from the shortest one in the front to tallest one in the back. Then the principal went up to the podium and gave a speech. Just imagine this going on every morning except for rainy or snowy days. The principal's speeches were criminally boring. I even felt sorry for him because he had to prepare something to say every morning even when he had nothing to say. I hated these assemblies, and I used every excuse I could come up with to avoid attending them. One good thing came out of getting hit by a pickup truck, besides meeting Harumi, of course, was that I had been excused from those assemblies. It seemed that somehow Harumi had been excused from them permanently. I didn't know why though.

"You know, Nobuo," as I was standing by the window and watching over the yard where the assembly was going on, Harumi came next to me, and said. "Those kids are making fun of you not because how you look, but because you react to what they say, you know?"

"I know; don't lecture me." I looked at Harumi's face. She was staring at me. "I can't help it. I can't control my anger."

"You must!" Harumi tried to hold my hand. I moved away. "I'll tell you why; when you attack those kids, you hurt me lot more than you hurt them."

"What?" I did not understand what Harumi was trying to tell me. "What do you mean? I've never hit you, have I?"

"No, you've never hit me," Harumi said slowly and calmly. "But when you get into fight, you make me very sad, and I feel so much pain in my heart. Do you understand?"

I didn't answer, but I sort of understood what she was saying.

"I know you are a smart and sweet kid. I know you are much more mature than all the other kids. I don't understand why you get upset so easily over things that are so unimportant." Harumi kept talking, and she was making me very uncomfortable. "You know what I am saying, don't you?"

A familiar march was blasted from the speakers in the yard, and the kids on the right line started marching into the building, then the next line, and then the next. I thought that the whole process was really ridiculous, and I was glad that I was not taking part in it.

Kids were coming into the classroom, so I went to my desk and sat down. Harumi was still standing by the window and watching me. I knew she was waiting for my answer.

There was a test on arithmetic in the morning. I used algebra to solve the problems and it was done very quickly. I opened a book on my lap and read it for the rest of the period.

I was still excused from going out to the yard after lunch, but I didn't want to stay in the classroom with Harumi, so I went out.

I walked around the cherry trees. The cherry blossoms were almost gone from the trees. I was feeling down. I couldn't pinpoint why but I was miserable. 'Is it really bad to react to what people say about you? I should not act on my feelings?' I was trying to think. 'If someone makes me angry, what am I supposed to do, nothing? Am I supposed to cry like a sissy?' Harumi asked me 'Why I get upset over something so unimportant?' 'But, is my pride unimportant? Are my feelings unimportant? What is important then?' 'Is it a crime to hit a kid when he does something bad or says something nasty to you? Then Mr. Yoshida is the worst criminal. How many kids does he hit a day?' My thoughts were racing around all over and I was getting frustrated.

'Maybe I don't know the difference between right and wrong. Maybe

43

I don't know anything.' After a while I began to doubt myself and somehow it took some weight off my shoulders, and I was feeling a little better. 'Maybe I am not as smart as I thought I was. I thought I knew everything, but maybe I am just a kid who doesn't know much.'

I leaned against the wire fence, and looked around the schoolyard. Kids were engaged in all kinds of activities. Some kids were just running around, some were playing catch, others were playing dodge ball, and some were jumping rope.... I felt kind of strange that I was completely out of it. I wasn't feeling lonely though. I just felt as if I were detached from reality. Then I thought of Harumi, and I hurried back to the classroom.

Harumi was sitting at the desk and reading a book as usual. She looked at me for a second and then her eyes went back to the book.

"I won't fight when you are around," I stood by her desk, and said to Harumi. "I don't wanna make you sad."

"Well, that's a little better, but not good enough." She kept her eyes on the book.

"Not good enough? What more do you want?" For a second, I felt like I was talking to my mother.

"You must promise me you won't fight with anyone."

I knew she was playing tough.

"Ever? I can't promise you that." I thought for a second, and continued. "I promise I will try not to fight with anyone."

"You must try very hard and then it's okay, I guess." Harumi smiled and changed the subject. "Have you finished the drawing?"

"No, not yet," I answered. I was having trouble with that drawing. I liked the composition and the surroundings, especially the water which came out very well, but Harumi's figure was rather flat, and didn't have life to it. "I think we must go back to the spot and do it again."

On the following Sunday, Harumi and I met at the corner at eleven o'clock. My mother made two rice balls stuffed with pickled plum and wrapped with seaweed, and broiled a small sun dried fish for my lunch. I took out a small sketchbook and the oil pastel set, and I put all in a canvas shoulder bag. Harumi was carrying the same red backpack on her back.

"I smell summer coming." When we got to the top of the dike, Harumi took a deep breath and said. It was a warm beautiful day.

"Smell summer?" I took a deep breath but did not smell anything in particular.

"I like summer. I want to swim in the river if I get better." Harumi's eyes were twinkling. "Can you swim?"

"Not really, but I can float," I said. "I am a balloon, you know."

"Ha, ha, ha...," Harumi opened her mouth and laughed the same clear sweet laugh. "I like that! You see, you can call yourself a balloon, then why do you get angry if somebody else calls you *Balloon*?"

I did not have an answer to that.

We walked toward the school for a while and I stopped at my favorite spot. There, the slope was gentler and longer than any other place and it was covered evenly by thick but short grass. It was the perfect place for rolling down. I took the canvas bag from my shoulder and threw it down to the bottom of the slope. I lay myself on the grass and pushed the ground with my arm. I was rolling down fast and my baseball cap flew away.

"Harumi, come down!" When I reached the bottom, without getting up, I called out. "Feels great, you know."

"I can't." Harumi was still standing on the top.

"Why not?" I yelled.

"I just can't," Harumi yelled back and started to walk down carefully. She picked up my cap on the way and came down to about six feet from where I was lying. She took her backpack from her shoulder and put it on

45

the ground with my baseball cap. She lay herself gently on the grass and rolled down slowly. Her body stopped right next me. She raised her upper body and then she put her head on my chest.

"Don't move." I tried to move away, but Harumi held my body tight. "I can hear the sound of your life."

"What, the sound of my life?"

"Yes, your indomitable heart, beating, beating, will keep beating for many, many years ...." Harumi was pressing her face to my chest tightly. Her long black hair was flowing down to my right shoulder.

"Do you want to hear my heartbeat?" Harumi asked.

"I can't hear anything," pressing my ear on her chest gently, I said. I felt Harumi's small bony chest, and I was afraid that my head would be too heavy and hurt her.

"The heart is on the left side of the chest, silly," said Harumi, holding my head with both hands, and moving herself a little, as she pressed my head hard to her chest. I still couldn't hear anything.

"Wow, this is pretty severe!" Harumi was touching my scar on my head with her fingers. "Does it hurt?"

"No, it doesn't." I raised my head and looked at Harumi's face. "Will you leave my scar alone please?"

"I must tell you something." Harumi put her arms around me and said, "I have a heart problem, and I will be having surgery in three weeks."

"What? What's wrong? You look fine though." Now I understood that was the reason she was excused from all physical activities in school.

"I have three more Sundays." Harumi was holding me so tight; it made me feel very uncomfortable. "Then, I might be gone."

"What do you mean, you might be gone?" I wiggled my body, and she loosened her hold a little.

"By accident, I overheard the doctor telling my mom it would be a very risky operation." Harumi's eyes were welling up. "This sort of surgery has never been performed in Japan, and the success rate of the operation is less than ten percent, but if I don't have an operation I won't live another year. That's what the doctor said."

I was in total shock. I did not know what to say to Harumi. I felt tears coming down on my cheeks. I freed myself from Harumi and sat up. I wiped my tears with my shirt sleeve. Just the thought that Harumi could be dead soon frightened me, and it was unbearable.

"Will you spend time with me all three Sundays?" Harumi sat up and leaned on my shoulder, and said.

"Of course, I will spend time with you every day if possible."

We stood up and picked up our stuff. Harumi put my baseball cap on my head. We went down to the bank of the river, and walked along the river to the place where I had done the drawing last Sunday. We sat on the grass, and decided to have lunch.

Harumi took out a lacquered wooden box from her backpack and opened the lid. Large sliced sushi-rolls were lined up neatly inside. She held the box with two hands and told me to pick some.

"You can feed me if you want," I said to Harumi with a smile. "I promise I won't bite your fingers."

"You eat it yourself." Harumi was laughing. "Your hands are still clean. "

I gave one of my rice balls to Harumi, and she ate it deliciously. She even had hot tea in a little thermos. It was such delightful lunch.

After we finished eating, Harumi went and sat on the same rock as she had sat on last time. I corrected her position a little, and I went to work. This time, I was only sketching Harumi in a small sketchbook. I did about ten sketches, and asked Harumi to look. Harumi picked several sketches she liked, but I wasn't happy with any one of them. Most of them showed the figure fairly accurately, but they all looked so artificial, no life. Looking at one of the sketches, I tried to show her why I didn't like it, and I rubbed the figure on the paper with the tip of my middle finger. The lines and details were blurred and colors were mixed and flattened. Then, something strange happened; the figure on the paper came alive.

I was fascinated by the fact that by taking away details and flattening the surface, you could actually bring the subject alive. I was excited, and now I couldn't wait to go home and finish the drawing.

When we got back to the top of the dike, Harumi asked me to carry her on my back. I was so happy that she asked me. At that moment, there was nothing more I wanted to do than give her a piggyback ride.

"You know, Nobuo," resting her head on my shoulder, Harumi whispered. "I'm not afraid of death; everybody dies someday, you know. But, I don't wanna die now because life is so wonderful; I am so happy and having so much fun every day. There is so much I wanna do. So many things I wanna learn, so many places I wanna go, so many books I wanna read. I wanna see you make a lot more paintings, wanna see how you grow up too. I wanna be alive because life is so, so beautiful....."

I wanted to say something to her but could not find the words. I felt a single teardrop falling on my cheek.

Raining Moon

Cleaning the classrooms was kids' duty, from the first graders to the six graders with no exceptions. Once a week, a group of five boys and five girls were assigned to clean their classroom and the hallway in front of the classroom. On each floor, there was only one four foot sink with two faucets, and there were five classrooms, so each class had to take turns. The class I belonged to was number three, and every Wednesday was our class's turn.

I was one of the five boys on duty. Everybody hated this. I asked Mr. Yoshida if I could be excused from the duty because I didn't feel my left arm and right leg were completely healed. Mr. Yoshida didn't believe me, but he excused me from hand mopping the floors anyway.

Usually we started with the boys pushing all the desks and chairs to the back of the room. Meanwhile girls went and got two buckets full of water and started hand mopping the hallway floor with a cleaning cloth made of an old summer kimono, old diapers or whatever used cotton rag was available. We mopped the floors on our hands and knees. There was no hot water, so in winter it was a brutal task.

When I was in the group, we did not move desks and chairs one by one. I pushed them in a row all at once. The other boys straightened up the fallen or knocked down desks and chairs. After we pushed everything to one side, it was our turn to mop the floor.

I came up with the idea of making it a race. Since I was excused from the mopping, I acted as a referee. I asked the four boys to line up in the front of the room with their cleaning cloths.

"Get set, go!" They lifted their legs and ran with the cleaning cloths in their hands.

The girls came into the room, and cheered. The winner was exempt from the next race. The third race was between the two losers. When we finished mopping one side of the room, we moved everything to the other side. This time, the girls wanted to join the race. We had never finished the job so quickly.

Harumi was, of course, exempt from this duty, and some girls were not happy about it. In general, most girls thought Harumi was treated with favor by teachers. Several girls got together and went to Mr. Yoshida and complained about her exemption from the cleaning duty. They were told that it was because of her health condition. Mr. Yoshida did not elaborate any further. It seemed Harumi did not know about those girls' ill feelings toward her, or possibly she was not paying any attention to them. She did not put much effort into developing friendships with any girls in the class either.

When I came out, Harumi was sitting on the bench near the main gate with a book in her hand and her backpack at her side. She stood up and smiled as I was coming.

"Have you been waiting for me?" I asked Harumi. She just nodded.

I helped her put her backpack on. I held her hand as we were going out the gate. I heard some girls giggling behind us. Strangely, it didn't bother me. Harumi looked at me and gave me a big smile.

"I finally finished the drawing last night," I said to Harumi.

"Really? How did it come out? Can I see it? When can I see it?" Harumi stopped in the middle of the street and held my hand with both her hands. She was tiptoeing. "Will you bring it to school tomorrow?" A bunch of girls were passing by, looking at us and some were whispering.

"I will bring it on Saturday," I said. "I want to show it to Mr. Okamoto also." We had a two-hour art class on Saturdays.

I brought the whole drawing pad to school. I skipped the morning assembly and showed the drawing to Harumi. Harumi loved it.

"Take it home today," I told Harumi. "I will bring it to your place with you after school."

"Oh, thank you. My parents will love it too, I know." Harumi was ecstatic, she was literally jumping up and down.

I had to wait through two boring classes to get to the art class. I couldn't wait to show the drawing to Mr. Okamoto. There was no special classroom for art. The art teacher just came around with a bunch of stuff in a cart and conducted the class. Mr. Okamoto covered the teacher's desk with colorful fabric, and set up a still life on it with some flowers in a tall glass vase, three old books and a small ceramic horse. We were told to either work on the still life, or draw a person next to us with pencils, oil pastel or watercolor. Mr. Okamoto distributed drawing paper which was the only art supply the school gave us. Drawing pencil, water-color paint, oil pastel or any other material, we had to bring ourselves. I didn't like the paper given to us, so I always brought my own sketchbook or drawing pad.

When the initial chaos was settled, I brought my drawing pad to Mr.

Okamoto. He looked at every drawing in the pad, and then took two sheets out of the pad. One was the drawing I had given to Harumi, and the other one was the view from the top of the dike of the Tama River, which was finished just before the accident. Both of them were done with oil pastel, which was my favorite medium then.

"I like them all, excellent! But those two are exceptional." Mr. Okamoto took them to the front and pinned them on the bulletin board, and asked the entire class to look at them. Mr. Okamoto did this often, but I hated it. It always made me embarrassed, rather than proud.

I spent the rest of the class drawing the still life Mr. Okamoto set up. The pattern of the fabric reminded me of a Matisse painting, and that woke up my desire to paint in oil.

It had been my dream to learn oil painting for quite some time. In fact, I had been saving money in a piggy bank for almost two years, hoping someday I would have enough money to buy an oil painting set. My parents never gave us a regular allowance, but when we did some errand for them, sometimes they gave us a little money. The New Year's present was huge to us. We children not only received a big chunk of money from our parents on New Year's Day, but also from every uncle and aunt who visited us or whom we visited. I had not spent a penny. I was saving it all in a porcelain piggy bank. But I knew that the oil painting set I wanted was so expensive, and I had no idea how many years it would take to save enough money.

Toward the end of the class, Mr. Okamoto came to me and told me about the national art competition for sixth graders. He said that the gold prize winners' works would be exhibited in the Tokyo Metropolitan Fine Arts Museum.

"I'd like to include your drawing, the one with a figure in our school entry." Mr. Okamoto was pointing at the drawing on the bulletin board.

"I gave the one with a figure to someone already," I said. "You could send the other one though, if you like."

"You gave it to someone, well......., I really want that one." Mr. Okamoto was staring at the drawing. "Do you think I could borrow it for the competition? All entries will be returned, so it will come back for sure."

"No, I don't think so," I said. There was no way I could take it away from Harumi now, I thought.

"I would love to see the drawing sent to the competition." Harumi was standing behind me. She must have overheard our conversation. I stared at her and tried to give her the signal by shaking my head. I really wanted Harumi to have the drawing. I didn't care about the competition.

"Thank you Harumi. I will personally make sure you will have it back after the competition," said Mr. Okamoto, "all right, Nobuo?" He didn't wait for my answer and walked away. I was not happy about it.

"I know you will win the gold prize." Harumi looked really excited. "Can I come with you to see the drawing in the museum then? How cool would that be!?"

It started to rain in the evening and soon it was pouring. It was Saturday night. I was worried about the next day. Harumi and I were supposed to meet at eleven o'clock at the corner. We did not talk about what we would do in case of rain. I had been planning on the idea; I wanted to make a drawing of the panoramic view from the top of the dike, using multiple sheets of paper. I thought Harumi could help me on this one. I figured that we would need three Sundays to complete the drawing.

It was still raining in the morning. As soon as I woke up, I became restless. We did not have a telephone, as a matter of fact, nobody I knew had one. The telephone was a real luxury then; you needed to buy an expensive government bond to have a phone installed in your house.

I didn't know what to do. I kept doing the same thing; walking around the house, looking out the windows, walking around the house, looking out the windows.

"Stop it, Nobuo!" my sisters were shouting, "you are driving us crazy!" They were studying at the small dining table on tatami.

"Sit down, Nobuo!" my mother kept yelling at me. "You cannot go to the river today. Sit down and read a book or do some painting!" To begin with, the house was too small for all of us to sit down and do something peacefully.

I decided that I would go to the corner anyway, whether Harumi would come or not. I knew I would go crazy if I stayed, and I would take everyone else down with me.

A little after ten o'clock, there was a knock on the front door. My mother answered. I could not recognize the woman's voice, but I heard she mentioned Harumi's name a few times and I knew it was Harumi's mother. They talked a few minutes and my mother came to me.

"Harumi's mother is inviting you for lunch at their house." My mother was all smiles. "Isn't that nice?"

I picked up a small sketchbook and the oil pastel set, and I was ready.

"Thank you, Nobuo. Thank you so much." Harumi's mother kept thanking me, and made me feel very awkward.

'Thank me for what?' I was thinking. 'She has absolutely no reason to thank me. She is rescuing me! I am the one who must thank her.'

Harumi's mother stopped in front of the iron gates hinged to two tall stone columns. She pushed the side door and gestured me to go in. There were irregularly shaped stepping stones imbedded in the ground which led to the house. Harumi was waiting outside of the sliding doors without an umbrella. I saw her smiling and tiptoeing.

"Harumi, you are getting wet!" her mother said with a worried expression on her face.

I folded the umbrella and placed it in the ceramic umbrella stand in the entryway. I took off my shoes and stepped up on the wooden floor. Harumi's father came to greet me.

"How do you do?" I knelt on the floor properly, put my hands in front of me on the floor, and bowed to the man. "Thank you for inviting me to your house, sir."

"Nobuo is so polite, isn't he?" Harumi's mother said.

I was led to a large room with a beautiful wooden floor with a white carpet in the center. On the carpet, there were two sofas and western style chairs arranged around a large, low glass table. I felt like I was in a foreign movie or something. This room alone was, I thought, larger than the whole house our family lived in.

I was asked to sit on the sofa. I had never sat on a sofa before. It was soft and I was extremely uncomfortable. Harumi sat next to me. Her mother sat across from us on a chair. Harumi's father left the room as soon as we sat down. Harumi and I looked at each other, and I was able to tell she was worried. She was worried because I looked as stiff as a log, and she knew I was uncomfortable.

A young woman with a white apron brought an iron tea pot, two small ceramic cups and Japanese pastries. I saw two big *daifuku* among other pastries all made with red beans on a bamboo plate.

"Please have some," Harumi's mother said gently. "You like sweets, don't you?"

I blushed. My mother told me often that I was fat because I ate too many sweets. There were two small forks made of ivory, but Harumi picked one of the pasties up with two fingers and brought to her mouth, and she bit a piece off. I took one of the *daifuku* and did the same. We looked at each other and smiled.

I noticed a grand piano in the corner of the room. It wasn't a huge one, but it was black, shiny and beautiful. A grand piano in a house! My two sisters had been taking piano lessons for some time, but we did not have a piano. They used a long narrow paper which had a piano keyboard printed on it to practice. They sometimes hummed the melody as their fingers moved on the printed keys. Both sisters started to learn at the same time, but my sister, Hisako was way ahead of my eldest sister, Michiko. Hisako was a natural musician. She had a perfect ear, and memorized the music at first glance. Michiko however was a very hard worker; she practiced a lot more than Hisako, and she was more serious about music than Hisako. Hisako was an easy going happy girl, and I loved her. She was two years older than I, but I felt like she was my younger sister.

"Do you play piano?" I asked Harumi.

"Yes, I just learned *For Elise*," Harumi said. "Do you wanna hear?"

"You mean Beethoven's?" I was surprised, and wondered; 'How many more surprises is this girl hiding?'

"Of course it's Beethoven's."

I was familiar with the music. Because of my mother's love for classical music, the only radio we had was tuned to the classical music station all day, every day.

Harumi played it quite beautifully. Harumi's mother and I applauded.

"Now I'll play more serious music," Harumi announced and started to play an old Japanese children's song. It was called "*amefuri otsuki-san*". It means *Raining Moon*. Harumi started to sing with her piano.

> *Raining Moon behind the cloud*
> *When you go for wedding, whom do you go with?*
> *I go alone with umbrella*
> *When there is no umbrella whom do you go with?*
> *Shala, Shala, Shang, Shang, bells attached, on horseback*
> *I go getting wet*

Harumi's clear sweet voice and simple melody somehow struck my heart, and I didn't know why, but I became a little sad.

"Nobuo, come here," without looking at me Harumi called. I went behind her.

"Sit down." Harumi made room for me to sit next to her.

"What children's song do you like?" asked Harumi. I thought about it a little, and I said that I liked *Red Dragonfly*. I sang as Harumi played piano.

"You have a beautiful voice!" still sitting on the chair Harumi's mother exclaimed. I had a loud voice like my mother, but I didn't have a beautiful voice like my mother.

We knew a lot of songs, and Harumi was able to play most of them on the piano. We sang one after another, as many as we knew. When we were running out of songs I turned around. Harumi's mother had her head resting on her hand, and she was crying. I thought it was strange because Harumi and I were having such a good time, and we were happy. I didn't understand what made Harumi's mother cry. As soon as she noticed that I was looking at her, she left the room.

"You wanna see my room?" Harumi stood up and asked.

"You have your own room?" I couldn't believe it. I couldn't even imagine a kid having his or her own room.

"Come." Holding my hand, Harumi led me down the hallway.

The room was not big but very clean and neat. It had a wood floor and one wall was covered with bookshelves. The most amazing thing was the bed which was placed near the window. I had never seen a bed outside of a hospital. There was a desk and chair with a lamp.

I admired the books on the bookshelves. My father's books were very old and had bulky hard covers. But Harumi's books were all new and looked pretty.

"My aunt works at a publishing company. She brings me books every time she visits us," Harumi said, and picked up a square book which was sitting on her desk. "She gave me this last week."

"Come and look!" She jumped up on the bed. It was a book of Paul Klee's paintings with the text written in a foreign language. I had seen Klee's works in reproduction, but there were a lot of images I hadn't seen before in the book. I sat next to Harumi, and we examined every page carefully.

There was a knock on the door, and Harumi's mother and the woman with the white apron came in. They were each carrying a tray.

"We brought some lunch for you," Harumi's mother said.

Harumi opened the fusuma door and went in. I didn't realize but there was another room right next to this one. It was a six tatami room with four shoji screens on one side.

There was a small low table in the center of the room. Harumi and I sat on the square futon mat facing each other. Curry on rice, shrimp tempura, and glasses of milk were on the trays. Harumi's mother opened the shoji screens, and a beautifully manicured Japanese garden appeared through the glass doors. It was still raining hard.

After lunch we looked at Klee's paintings again. It inspired me to draw some pictures.

"Let's make a drawing together," I suggested. "I brought a sketchbook."

I remembered that I left my sketchbook and oil pastel set on the sofa.

"Stay here, I'll go and get them." Harumi stood up and went out of the room.

Harumi was taking a long time so I looked at the garden, and for a moment I felt as if I were dreaming. I wondered if I had been brought to another world by some magic. The constantly falling rain drops were forming a veil, and it was protecting me from reality.

"Here you are." Finally Harumi came back with my sketchbook and oil pastel. "But this is too small for us to work together. I asked dad to give us a larger sheet of paper."

Harumi's father brought us a thick water color paper almost half the size of the table. Harumi went to the next room and got two drawing pencils, a set of water colors, a large metal palette, and several different size brushes.

We decided to create an imaginary island with lots of stuff. It was Harumi's idea. I drew a large irregular circle on the paper with pencil, and we were all set to work.

At first, we drew images with pencils. I worked on the ocean surrounding the island; whales and all sizes and shapes of fishes, seaweed and shells. Harumi was drawing a town with lots of houses and trees, and a school building. She was really good. Then I made a zoo with different animals. Harumi worked on a playground with slides, sand box and a bunch of children. After we finished drawing, Harumi went and got some water in a bottle, and we started to color the images. We used both oil pastels and water colors. We were so absorbed in the painting that we totally lost a sense of time.

"Oh my goodness, it's so wonderful!" Harumi's mother came in to see what was happening and screamed. She must have been curious because we were so quiet for so long. "I must get your father to see this."

"Done!" Harumi and I said in unison. We had filled the entire paper with colorful images. We had completed the project.

"Wait a minute," said Harumi, and using a black oil pastel, drew a small umbrella in the right bottom corner of the painting, and signed her name on one side of the handle. "Now you must write your name on the other side." I did exactly that.

"We are lovers now," Harumi declared.

"Lovers?" I didn't get it. "What do you mean?"

"You see, this is a sign for lovers." She was pointing at the umbrella. "I saw it in an old story book."

Harumi's mother and father rushed into the room.

"Wow, this is amazing!" Looking at the painting, father exclaimed, "You guys did a wonderful job! We must frame this."

"You see this?" pointing the umbrella Harumi said. "We are lovers."

Harumi's parents burst into laughter.

RAINBOW

"Nobuo, you must attend physical education classes from now on," Mr. Yoshida told me as he was leaving the classroom after lunch. "The team needs you too."

Because of the accident, I had been excused from physical education classes. The team he was referring to was our class's baseball team.

Most of the Japanese schools have adopted the trimester system. The first term is from April to July. August is summer vacation. The second term is from September to December, and the third term is from January to March.

Every year in the middle of June, from fourth grade up, we had baseball tournaments for boys, and volleyball tournaments for girls. These were elimination tournaments among classes of the same grade. The children as well as teachers, the whole school took the events very seriously. From early May, we did our training and practice during the physical education classes.

I was a catcher, mainly because nobody wanted to play the position. We were using a ball made of rubber instead of a regular baseball which was made of cork wrapped with rubber strings and leather. The rubber baseball was invented in Japan to encourage small children to play baseball. It was a little softer and safer for kids to play with, but still, catcher was a tough position. The only protective gear for the catcher was the mask. We didn't have helmets or uniforms; we just played with whatever we were wearing that day. The school had some equipment, like home plate and bases, bats and balls, and some gloves. Most of the gloves were made of heavy canvas stuffed with straw and cotton, and were worn out. The catcher's mitt was also made in the same manner, and was in bad shape, showing some straw from the seam. Some kids brought their own gloves from home. I had one made of pigskin, but didn't have a catcher's mitt. The catcher's mitt was too expensive. The pigskin glove was less flexible than the leather made, and more difficult to use, but it was cheaper.

I was hitting fourth in the batting order; I was supposed be a power hitter. I hit long balls occasionally, but I got struck out a lot. We had one good pitcher, his name was Hiroshi. Our team's performance was largely dependent on him. When he was good, we usually won the game.

We always did stretch exercises at the beginning of the physical education class, after which Mr. Yoshida told us to run around the schoolyard twice. I barely finished one round when I realized I was in trouble; my legs were getting tired and I was breathing heavily. I had to sit down on the ground. I never had such trouble before. I was big but I had never been slow and I was fairly athletic.

"What's the matter?" Mr. Yoshida called out. "You are in bad shape, Nobuo. Get up and go!"

I got up and managed to jog around the yard one more time. Then, Mr. Yoshida ordered me to run around the yard twice during lunch break, every day. I wasn't happy about it but I knew I had no choice.

On the following Saturday, after school, we had a practice game against the next class, Class Four team. Neither team was playing well; there were lots of errors and running mistakes. I made a terrible error also; a passed ball and a run scored. I had problems catching Hiroshi's pitches. He told me that he had mastered a breaking ball. He tried it with me before the game but I had trouble catching it. So I told him not to use it in the game until I got used to it. But when we were ahead in the game, he started to use it to show off. His slow curve ball was extremely effective for batters, but I just could not catch it.

Since it was a practice game, we played only six innings. At the bottom of the last inning, we were winning five to four. It was two out and the runners were on second and third. Hiroshi had been pitching fairly well, and wasn't showing any slowdown. He had one ball and two strikes against the batter. One more strike, and the game would be over. He went for a strike and the batter swung the bat. The bat hit the ball and the ball bounced back to the pitcher's mound. Hiroshi calmly caught the ball. He took a few steps toward first base and threw the ball.

The ball flew way over the first baseman's head and two runs were scored. We lost the game. I could not believe my eyes. Hiroshi looked stunned and could not move for a while. I heard loud gasps, and some boos from our classmates who were watching the game.

Hiroshi was walking toward the home plate with his head down. I went and put my arm around his shoulder, but he violently shrugged my arm off and walked away.

"It's all right, just a practice game," Mr. Yoshida said to Hiroshi, but he didn't even look back. Mr. Yoshida started to gather the equipment, and a few of us helped him in silence.

All the girls were either playing or watching the volleyball game at the other end of the schoolyard, but I saw Harumi watching our baseball game from afar on a bench. We met at the main gate. We walked for a while without a word.

"Is winning so important?" suddenly Harumi looked at me and asked.

"I think so," I said. "We play to win, so winning is very important." Then I asked her, "did you see it, Hiroshi's...?"

"Yes I did, and I thought something was wrong there." Harumi tilted her head a little and continued. "Why did he act like that? You tried to comfort him but were brushed off."

"Well, he didn't want any sympathy, I guess, or he was just embarrassed. I don't know."

"You made an error, didn't you?" Harumi said with grin on her face. "You allowed a run. How did you feel?"

"I felt bad, but....." I tried to remember, but I didn't know if I even felt bad. "It's different..."

"How is it different?" Harumi was persistent.

"I didn't lose the game." As I was saying it, I knew I wasn't giving the right answer.

"Do you think Hiroshi lost the game by himself?" I felt I was being interrogated.

"No, the team lost the game, because of his error."

"If you didn't make an error, the game could've ended in a tie, isn't that right?"

That was a good point. Harumi was trying to tell me that the game must be looked at with perspective. It is always true that errors and mistakes are a part of the game, just like the umpires' bad calls. There is no reason to blame anyone or anybody or to take it personally. I thought I would have a discussion with Hiroshi about that.

We were at the corner. We promised to meet there at eleven o'clock the next day. I told her about my plan; together we would make a drawing of panoramic views from the top of the dike, using multiple sheets of paper. Harumi liked the idea, but she pointed out that we would not have enough time to finish it before her operation. She asked me if I could wait for her to come back from the hospital to do it. I was so happy to hear that. Harumi would come back, and we would make a spectacular drawing.

It turned out to be a beautiful morning. I decided to make a small study for the panoramic drawing. So, in the canvas bag I put a small sketch book, two pencils and the usual lunch; two rice balls and roasted sun dried fish, and headed out. Harumi was waiting for me at the corner.

We walked on the path on top of the dike looking around to find a good place to do a drawing. I wanted to include the bridge over the river with the freight train on it in the scene. The train had to be a *Home Run*; when the train covered the entire bridge we called it a *Home Run*.

Harumi suggested that the bridge and the river must be in the center of the drawing, and we should use three sheets of paper. I thought that was a good idea.

We came to the spot where we saw some factory buildings on the left across the river, and the bridge with little forest like greens in the background, and a lot of small houses among the trees on the right. We could have the river snaking around from the upper right side to the lower left side on the center sheet.

"This is perfect," Harumi said. "This is perfect!" I repeated with excitement.

We sat on the slope near the top of the dike. I was wondering where I should start, left, right or the center part.

"Can I read you the Andersen book?" Harumi took a small book out from her little red backpack. "I only read the half of it last time."

"Yeah, sounds great," I screamed. "He lives! He lives!"

I decided to work on the center sheet first, and as I was starting to draw,

Harumi began reading.

Fifteenth Evening

I knew a Pulcinello, said the moon. The folks all shouted whenever he made his appearance on the stage. All his movements were comical, and raised peals of laughter in the house, although there was nothing in particular to call it forth, - it was only his oddity. Even when a mere lad, romping about with the other boys, he was a Pulcinello. Nature formed him for the character, by putting a hump upon his back and another on his chest. But the mind that was concealed beneath this deformity was, on the contrary, richly endowed. No one possessed a deeper spirit, than he. The stage was his world of ideals: had he been tall and handsome, every manager would have hailed as his first tragedian. All that was heroic and great filled his soul, and still his lot was to be a Pulcinello. His very sorrow, his melancholy, heightened the dry comicality of his sharply - marked features, and aroused the laughter of a ticklish public, who applauded its favorite.

The lonely Columbine was good and kind to him, and yet she preferred to give her hand to Harlequin. It would indeed have been too comical a thing in reality if "beauty and Beast" had married. Whenever Pulcinello was dejected, she was the only one who could bring a smile upon his face, but she could even make him laugh outright. At first she was melancholy like him, then somewhat calmer, and at last overflowing with fun. "I know well enough what ails you," she said; "it is love, and love alone!" And then he could not help laughing. "Love and I!" he exclaimed; "that would be droll indeed: how the folks would clap and shout!"

"It is love alone," she repeated with a comical pathos; "you love – you love me!"

Ay, people may speak thus when they imagine that in others' hearts there is no love. Pulcinello skipped high into the air, and his melancholy was gone. And yet she spoke the truth: he did love her; he loved her truly, fervently, as he loved all that was noble and beautiful in art. On her wedding-day he seemed the merriest of the merry; but in the night he wept: had the folks seen his wry face, they would have clapped their hands.

Not long ago Columbine died. On the day when she was buried, Harle-

quin had leave not to appear upon the boards: was he not a mourning widower? But the manager had to give something very merry, that the public might the less miss the pretty Columbine and agile Harlequin. So the nimble Pulcinello had to be doubly merry: he danced and skipped about – despair in his heart – and all clapped their hands and cried, "Bravo, bravissimo!" Pulcinello was called for. Oh, he was beyond all price!

Last night, after the performance, little Humpback strolled out the town, toward the lonely churchyard. The wreath of flowers upon Columbine's grave had already faded. There he sat down – it was a perfect picture – his chin resting upon his hand, his eyes turned toward me – a Pulcinello upon the grave, peculiar and comical.

Had the forks seen their favorite, how they would have clapped and cried, "Bravo, Pulcinello! Bravissimo!"

"It's so sad," I said. "How can I work listening to such a sad story?"

"Sad, but it's a beautiful story." Harumi was calm. She turned around to me and asked. "Do you love me?"

"I don't know," I said, quite surprised by the strange question. "I have no idea."

"If, *it is love and love alone*, I must know what love is and I want to know now." Harumi looked very serious. "There are love stories or stories about love in almost every book I read. But I don't quite get it."

"Ask your mother." I knew it was a stupid thing to say but I didn't know what else to say.

"I did," Harumi said. "You know what she said? She said I would know when I grow up; love is something I must experience. Isn't that a terrible answer? She knows I might not have time to grow up."

"Well, I thought you knew." I just remembered the umbrella she drew. "You said we were lovers."

"That was on the paper, not real." Harumi looked down. There was awkward silence for some time.

"Let's go by the river and have lunch," I said and stood up. Harumi put the book in the backpack. I held her hand, and we walked down the slope slowly.

We sat in the grass and were eating when I felt something jump by my left leg. Instinctively I covered it with my palm, gently picked it up and held it with both hands.

"What is it?" Harumi tried to look in my hands. I slowly opened my hands a little.

It was a tiny little green frog with big brown eyes. I opened the hands a little more, but the frog was still motionless.

"Oh, poor thing," looking inside of my hands Harumi whispered, "he must be terrified."

"Poor thing?" I looked at her and said. "It's so tiny and pretty, I want to take it home."

"No Nobuo, let him go," said Harumi, and put her hands on my arm. "The frog lives here; this is his home. He must have family or friends here too."

I gently put my hands on the grass and opened them, but the frog did not move. It looked like the frog was examining us. I slowly separated my hands, and the frog fell, then it jumped and disappeared in the grass.

"Will you read me more stories from the Andersen book?" I said to Harumi. I lay down. I didn't feel like drawing any more.

Harumi started to read and I closed my eyes. Her voice sounded like music and the stories took me to faraway lands.

"Are you listening or sleeping?" after reading three stories, Harumi bent over my face, and asked.

"Yes, I am listening, and I am in heaven." I raised my both arms in the air.

"I don't think it's fair." Harumi made a face. "Since you are not drawing, you should read to me as well."

We agreed to read it alternately. When I read, Harumi lay down and closed her eyes, just as I did when she was reading. I glanced at her, eyes closed and her long black hair spread over the grass like an open fan. She looked stunningly beautiful.

We came to the last story of the book. It was my turn to read.

Thirtieth Evening

I will tell you which occurred a year ago, said the Moon, in a country-town in the south of Germany. The master of a dancing-bear was sitting in the tap-room of an inn, eating his supper; while the bear, poor harmless beast was tied up behind the woodstack in the yard.
In the room upstairs three little children were...

It was a nice little story, and when I finished reading, I lay down next to Harumi and held her hand. In the blue sky with no cloud, we were floating and slowly going higher and higher. How long had we stayed like that, I did not know.

We raised ourselves eventually, and we walked on the trail along the river heading home. The water was high and flowing rapidly. We came upon a field where many little yellow flowers were blooming. Harumi and I each picked a handful of flowers. I cut off a thin weed on the ground and tied the stems of flowers and made a little bouquet. We were back on the trail. I tried to place my little bouquet in Harumi's hair, but the flowers came loose and scattered around Harumi's shoulder. Harumi smiled and I laughed out loud.

We heard some rustling sound in the grass and looked. There were a man and a woman lying on the grass embracing each other. They raised their heads and looked at us. I felt as if I had witnessed something I should not have, and kept walking. Harumi stopped and stared at them for a few seconds.

"They were making love," Harumi whispered in my ear.

"Is that what it is?" I was wondering why she was hung up on this thing, *love* so much?

The trail was branching out leading to the dike. We walked down quietly to the stone steps on the slope. As soon as we climbed up to the top,

I crouched down and Harumi climbed onto my back.

"Hey, look!" As I was standing up with Harumi on my back, I saw a rainbow in the distance. It was not big, but it looked amazing with colors so bright and distinctive.

"How beautiful!" Harumi whispered.

"Harumi, you will be all right," I said with conviction. "The rainbow is a sign of hope, and seeing it is good luck, you know, I read it somewhere."

"I hope so," Harumi uttered softly. "I hope so, Nobuo."

Four-Leaf Clover

The after school homework gang had been expanding. Now five of us regularly stayed and worked on the homework together. The first kid who came to us after Harumi was Yousuke. I did not like him; the way he talked, the way he acted, he wasn't a straight forward person. I thought he was a kind of manipulative, sneaky kid. I just didn't like him. He was hanging around us for a few days, but I ignored him. It was Saburo who asked him if he wanted to join us. Yousuke was of course delighted, and said yes.

"I don't know about that," I said to Saburo. "I want to keep it for just three of us; if the group becomes bigger, Kamikaze sensei will notice, and who knows what he would do."

"He should know about us by now," Harumi intervened. "I think we should welcome anyone who wants to join us."

"Anyone?" feeling a little betrayed, I said to Harumi.

"Yes anyone," Harumi said it like a declaration. "This is not even a club or anything. We are just staying in the classroom after school and doing homework. Anyone could do the same. Nobody needs anyone's permission."

I wanted to point out to Harumi that not long ago she asked us, Saburo and me, if she could join, and we gave her permission. But I swallowed the words. Deep down, I knew that Harumi and Saburo were right. I did not want to push them to say if I didn't like it I could leave. Two against one, and I sensed that Harumi was determined. Yousuke was very happy.

About a week later, Saburo brought a girl who was not even in our class. Her name was Kyoko, and she was a Korean. This time I did not object because Saburo did talk to me and Harumi about her beforehand. Kyoko was way behind us academically. She had just started to attend our school. Before this, she had been homeschooled.

One afternoon, after we finished our homework, Saburo asked me if we could talk. We went to the river, and Harumi came along. We sat on the slope near the top of dike, and Saburo told us what had been happening in the village lately.

Mr. Yoshida came to the village a few times in the evening, and talked to the elders who represented the people in the village. As a result, there was a meeting between Mr. Yoshida and the parents who had school age children. Mr. Yoshida was trying to encourage those parents to send their children to school. They were not Japanese citizens, so they had no legal obligation to send their children to school, and quite often the schools were reluctant to accept them. Mr. Yoshida told them that the school principal guaranteed that every child who wanted to come would be accepted, and he was wholeheartedly willing to work with Mr. Yoshida to make sure that their children would have a happy and successful education at the school. However, Mr. Yoshida was not very successful convincing the Korean parents. The parents were afraid that even if their children were accepted to school, they would be picked on or bullied by Japanese children, and they would have a miserable time in school. They also told Mr. Yoshida that they had their community schooling system, however primitive and ineffective it was. Mr. Yoshida was persistent, didn't want to give up, and went to the village several times to talk to parents individually. Finally there was another village meeting, and Mr. Yoshida invited five Korean children including Saburo who were attending school to talk about their experiences in school. That seemed to have had some effect, and a group of children started to come to school.

Kyoko was one of them. The evaluation test showed Kyoko's academic level was about fourth grade, but she was put in the sixth grade because of her age.

Japanese compulsory education has always been age oriented. By law, parents have an obligation to send their children to school for a period of nine years, from the first April 1, after a child's sixth birthday until the first March 31, after the child's fifteenth birthday. There are no skipping grades or repeating grades, period.

"You helped me, Nobuo, that's why I am doing okay," Saburo said. "Now, it's my turn to help someone."

"Saburo, that's wonderful," Harumi said excitedly, and then mumbled. "Kamikaze sensei is not a bad person after all." That was what I was thinking.

Kyoko was a Saburo's cousin and living in the village with her mother who was a widow. She was placed in class number one which was two doors away from our class. There were no computers or copy machines those days, so teachers used mimeographs to make all tests and homework sheets; they scratched letters and characters on waxed stencil and placed it around an ink-fed drum and printed them by hand. Because of this time consuming tedious work, they used the same tests and homework sheets for all five classes. So, quite often the homework Kyoko was assigned was exactly the same as ours. Kyoko was quiet and timid, but eager to learn. Harumi became her tutor; in fact, she was a tutor to everyone. Whenever Yousuke had trouble he asked Harumi. Saburo too went to Harumi for help rather than coming to me. Harumi was very gentle and patient with everyone. I thought it was strange that I became a kind of outsider in something I started. Occasionally Harumi gave me mock tests for writing Kanji.

Wednesday was our class cleaning day. We could not stay in the classroom so we decided to go to the river. There was no such thing as a library in the school. We tried to do homework on the dike, but it was a little windy, and we could not keep the page of the social studies textbook open. We gave up the idea of doing homework, so instead we played. Saburo, Yousuke and I rolled down the slope a few times. Then we decided to make it a race. Saburo won every time, way ahead of Yousuke and me. I could not figure out how he did it. I was the slowest one.

Harumi and Kyoko were searching for four-leaf clovers. Clovers with four leaves were rarities and considered lucky. Three boys joined them for the search.

"I found it!" Yousuke screamed.

We all gathered around him and looked, it had five leaves.

"Can't you even count to five?" I said jokingly and everyone laughed.

We were looking for quite some time, and Harumi suggested that we should give up and head home. As I was going back up the slope, I saw it; the four-leaf clover was proudly sticking its head out of the grass. Everybody else was already on top of the dike. Slowly and carefully I put my thumb and pointer on the stem and snatched it off. Then I gently put it in my shirt pocket.

Saburo and Kyoko went down the slope toward the school, and Yousuke, Harumi and I took the path on the dike. I was waiting for Yousuke to leave. I knew he would have to turn at the street below before us. Waiting was very frustrating. I was worried how the clover was surviving. As soon as Yousuke hopped down the stone steps, I peeked into my breast pocket. It was still there and wasn't getting squashed. I stopped, and put my thumb and pointer into the pocket very carefully.

"What are you doing?" walking ahead of me, Harumi turned around

74

and asked.

"This is for you." I pulled out the four-leaf clover and stretched my arm and showed it to her. Harumi looked puzzled for a second, and then examined it carefully.

"Four-leaf clover!" Harumi covered her mouth with both hands and screamed. "Where did you find it? Why didn't you tell us?"

"It's for you," I said. "I wanted to give you good luck, I wanted to make it a surprise."

"Thank you, it's so beautiful," said Harumi. She then picked it up with her fingertips. "You are so sweet."

We walked for a while without a word. Harumi kept her eyes on the clover.

"I like you very much." Harumi looked at me with a sweet smile.

"I like you too." I smiled back.

The next morning I came to school a little late. Students were already lined up for the assembly, and the principal was coming up to the podium.

"This morning, I have good news to report." The principal was unusually upbeat. "We have a hero in the school. His name is Saburo Kaneda, he is a sixth grader, in Mr. Yoshida's class."

Some kids were turning their heads and looking at Saburo. I could not see his face but he looked as stiff as a log from the back.

"Yesterday, after school on his way home, Saburo found a bag by the rear gate." The principal continued. "He opened it and there was money inside, lots of money. Without any hesitation, he brought it to my office. It turned out that the money was this month's salary for the teachers and staff of the school." There were murmurs and whispers among the kids.

Japan was, in those days, a cash society. There were no credit cards or personal checks; most of the transactions, business or personal, were done in cash. Salaries were paid monthly in cash also. Every month, small armored cars delivered cash from banks to the businesses, factories, schools and so forth.

"Saburo is a Korean, he came to Minemachi Elementary School this year." The principal continued. "But already he has learned one of the most important things in life; integrity. I am very proud of him. I am also proud of our school where you children and we teachers together, create such a nurturing environment." I thought it sounded like a politician's election year speech. There were several flashes during the speech. Someone must have been taking pictures. At the end of the speech, the principal asked all the children to applaud Saburo.

We began marching back to our classrooms. The principal came down and went directly to Saburo and took him away from the line.

Saburo came back to the classroom half way into the first period. He did not look happy at all. He had angry expression on his face.

"What's the matter?" I whispered.

"Later," said Saburo and turned his face to the blackboard.

There was a ten minute break between classes. During the break I tried to talk to him, but he repeatedly said 'not now, later'.

"Can I see you by the cherry trees?" finally, after lunch he spoke to me.

"I have to do two running laps," I said to Saburo. "Kamikaze is watching me."

"I'll wait for you."

After a week of running every day, I was getting strength back in my legs, and no longer collapsed on the ground after one lap. Saburo was sitting alone on the bench.

"I didn't learn to be honest in this school." Saburo was angry. "Did you hear what the principal said? Does he think all Koreans are thieves?"

"I wasn't paying much attention," I said, although I did hear what the principal said.

"I'll tell you what happened," said Saburo glancing at me, and then he looked at the ground. "Yesterday, Kyoko and I parted from you guys and were walking along the wire fence of the school. We were passing by the rear gate and we saw a bag sitting there, but I didn't pay attention. It was Kyoko who went and checked it out, and called me. I looked inside the bag and I was shocked to death. I'd never seen so much money in my life. I blanked out and didn't know what to do. Then, Kyoko said I should bring it to the principal's office. So I took it to the principal's office. The office was in chaos, I heard someone say they had received a wrong payroll bag, or something. Then, they treated me like I saved their lives. I tried to explain to the principal and everyone there, it wasn't me who found the bag, but it was Kyoko. Nobody wanted to listen. Meanwhile Kyoko was still waiting for me at the gate."

"Can you believe it? They didn't even let me leave the room." Saburo raised his head and looked at me. "I wanted to go and get Kyoko, or at least tell her what was happening there."

"Why didn't they let you leave the room?" I asked.

"I don't know. They said the police had been called, and the bank people were coming over, therefore I could not leave." Saburo took a deep breath. "I had to yell at the principal, and then finally he paid attention to me. The principal and I went to the gate, and we saw two police officers coming in, but Kyoko wasn't there."

Volleyball came rolling down slowly to Saburo's feet. Saburo picked it up and threw it to a girl who was standing in the distance.

"The case is closed. As far as the principal was concerned; Kyoko didn't exist. When the policeman asked me, I told him exactly what happened; Kyoko found the bag and told me to bring it there, and so on. He wrote down everything, but then, you know what he said? Since I brought the bag in, I would receive the reward. Reward? If anyone deserves a reward, it's Kyoko. To be honest with you, Nobuo, I don't know what I would have done if Kyoko hadn't told me to bring it to the principal's office. I might have just brought it home. Especially after I heard the principal's speech, I thought maybe I should have kept the money. I learned *integrity* in this school?"

"I think it was stupid for him to say such a thing," I said to Saburo. "It shows he is basically a racist. But the fact is, you could have taken the money, but you didn't. You didn't have to listen to Kyoko, but you did. That's all that matters. You did the right thing."

There was a bell; it was time to go back to the classroom.

"After the assembly, I was taken to the principal's office and had to meet the reporters from the newspapers," as we were standing up, Saburo said. "They took a picture of me and the principal, but the principal did all the talking, I couldn't tell them what really happened."

"How does Kyoko feel about it?" I thought it was an important question. "Is she annoyed you got all the credit and attention, and she wasn't even mentioned in the speech?"

"On the contrary, she is very happy and amused that she escaped all the attention." Saburo was laughing. "You know, she left the gate and went home because she saw the policemen coming. She told me. She thought we were in big trouble."

"Then, what's the problem?" I said with a grin. "If Kyoko is okay with it, then what are you complaining about? Get over it!"

SUN PRINCESS

We did not have homework on Saturdays, but there were arithmetic and science tests scheduled on Monday, so everyone wanted to stay and study after school, everyone, except me. I did not need to study for the tests, but since Harumi wanted me to stay, I stayed. I decided to work on the watercolor painting I could not finish during the art class. I bought a new kind of watercolor paint which I could use as ordinary watercolor by thinning it with water. But also I could apply it thickly on paper and get an oil painting look. And, the color would not crack after it dried. I loved this new discovery.

Harumi was, as usual, helping others. She looked so happy and she seemed to enjoy doing so. I didn't get it. She told me that she would not be in school from Monday on because she would have to see doctors and have all sorts of tests in the hospital even before she would be admitted on Wednesday. The operation was scheduled on Thursday. Yet, she wanted to help others to prepare for the tests.

"Is this the new paint you told me about?" After everyone settled down, Harumi came over and looked at my painting. "I like it. It looks like an oil painting, so cool."

"Yeah, I love it," I said. "I think we should use this on the panorama painting when you come back."

"Nobuo, will you stop by my house this afternoon?" asked Harumi in a whisper. "I won't be able to see you tomorrow, so I want to spend some time with you today."

"Why can't you see me tomorrow?" I was so disappointed. "We promised."

"My mother asked my uncle and aunt to come and stay with us until my operation is over; they are arriving from Kobe tomorrow." Harumi said. "My uncle is a doctor, you know; mother thinks he will give us moral support."

"Sure, I would love to come to your house, of course," I said, trying to sound like I was excited. Harumi gave me a soft smile.

I wanted to be with Harumi, but I was not particularly looking forward to going back to Harumi's house. Although it was a wonderful place, somehow I could not relax there. I also knew Harumi and her mother tried very hard to make me comfortable, but the harder they tried, the more uncomfortable I became.

As Harumi opened the glass sliding door to the house, I faced the drawing Harumi and I had made last Sunday on the wall, instead of the old Chinese painting on the silk scroll which was there last time. The drawing was in an elaborate gold leaf frame with silk matting, the kind you normally see on the old master paintings in the museum. It looked good, but somehow it made me feel embarrassed.

"Ojama-shimasu," I said. I took my backpack off my shoulder, knelt on the wood floor and bowed to Harumi's father and mother. It meant 'Allow me to disturb you.' My mother had taught me to say it whenever visiting someone's house.

"Not at all, we have been expecting you," Harumi's father said. "Please come in."

"Thank you so much for coming," Harumi's mother said. "We are so happy you are here."

While all this greeting was going on, Harumi disappeared. I was led to the living room and sat on the sofa. The woman with a white apron came and put two glasses of orange juice and some cookies on the table. With Harumi's mother's urging, I picked up the glass and tasted the orange juice. Orange juice was a luxury in Japan. I had it only once before when my grandfather took me to the theater and treated me in the café on the way home. I liked it very much.

Harumi's father left the room but her mother sat across from me on the chair.

"What do you think?" Out of nowhere, Harumi appeared standing in front of me wearing a bright yellow dress, as bright as the sun. "Do you like it?"

"Wow, pretty!" I said and then added. "You look like a sun princess."

"Sun princess? I like that," Harumi laughed. "I am going to wear this to the hospital on Wednesday." Harumi picked up the flared skirt with her fingertips and made a complete turn.

"Will you dance with me, Nobuo?" tilting her head a little Harumi asked.

"No, I don't know how to dance," I answered instantly.

"I'll show you how..., please?" Harumi looked at her mother. She was smiling but quickly stood up and left the room. I shook my head sideways a few times. I really did not want to dance.

"Please stand up." Harumi came and held my hands. I reluctantly got up and followed her off the white carpet. She put my right hand on her waist and held my left hand with her right hand.

"We need some music," she said and let go of my hand.

"I don't want to dance," I said to her and made a face.

"Oh, you are so unromantic." Harumi looked disappointed. It was the second time she called me that. 'What's romantic?' I wondered, still had no idea.

"Let's go to my room," said Harumi, and headed to the hallway. I picked up my backpack and followed.

We sat in the tatami room. The shoji screens were opened showing the garden through the glass doors, which made me feel like I was in a wonderland again. Harumi brought some new books her aunt had given her; a poetry book by some French poet and a few novels by well-known Japanese authors. None of them was interesting to me, and I asked for the book of Klee's paintings. Harumi brought the book and sat next to me. We looked at each picture carefully and talked about what we saw in the paintings. The more I looked at Klee's paintings, the more I was fascinated by the dreamlike world he created, and I thought I should try to make some paintings in his style.

"Can we make a drawing like Klee?" I said to Harumi and took out a small sketchbook from my backpack.

"You do it, I'll watch," said Harumi and moved to the side of the table.

Using oil pastel, I drew a rainbow in the center first and then, a long freight train on top of the rainbow. Underneath, I made a field of green, blue and yellow stripes. I took out my pencil box from my backpack and found a paperclip. I scratched four-leaf clovers on the field with the paperclip, many of them. Harumi was quietly watching me while I was working on it.

"This is for your good luck," I said. "I want you to take it with you to the hospital."

I looked at her face and saw tears in her eyes. Before I could say anything she stood up and opened the glass doors.

"I don't want to go," Harumi whispered.

"Go where? I said. A cool breeze swept into the room and wrapped my whole body.

"I don't want to go to the hospital." Harumi was sobbing. "I know I won't come back."

"What do you mean, you won't come back?" I yelled and stood up.

Harumi grabbed my arm, put her face on my shoulder and cried. "I know I will die if I have the operation."

"Don't go then," I said. "Why do you have to go s if you know it won't work?"

"Nobody listens to me. My dad, mom, uncle and the doctor, all say I have a better chance of surviving if I have the operation."

"We should run away," I said. "You and I should go someplace far away."

"How can we go away?" Harumi looked at my face. "Where can we go?"

"I don't care where, someplace far away. You know the freight train that runs on the bridge over the Tama River. I hear it slows down just before the bridge and some people take free rides on it." I was getting excited with my idea. "We could do that. I have some money in a piggybank too."

There was a knock on the door and her mother came in with tea and Japanese pastries.

"Did you just draw this?" looking at the drawing she said with excitement. "What a beautiful work!"

"Nobuo made it for me," Harumi said. "He wants me to take it to the hospital for good luck."

"How sweet of you, Nobuo," she said blinking her eyes rapidly. "You've been so nice to my daughter."

Harumi's mother asked me to stay for dinner. She said she would go and get permission from my mother. I told her I wanted to go home. Harumi came to the gate to see me off.

"Why can't you stay for dinner?" Harumi said.

"I just want to go home," I said without looking at her.

"What are you going to do tomorrow? Harumi asked.

"Usual....," I said. "I will go to the river and work on the study for the panorama painting."

I woke up with a little headache in the morning. I was feeling down and did not want to do anything. I was not feeling better after lunch and wondered if I should go to the river or not. My two little brothers wanted to play wrestling with me. I told them no, but they attacked me anyway, so I went along and played around making a racket. Mother kept yelling at us to be quiet. I decided to go and work on the sketch anyway. It was already after three o'clock.

It was a little windy but a nice warm day. Walking on the dike toward the place where we had decided to do the painting, I thought about Harumi. 'How does she know she is going to die if she has the operation?' I wondered. 'Why can't she refuse, if she doesn't want to go?' It appeared to me that her parents would do anything for her. I didn't think her parents would force her to have the operation.

In the distance, I saw the freight train crossing the bridge. Somehow it looked further away than usual. I had never gone close to the bridge. 'I should go and check it out someday.' I thought. I wanted to see how the train slowed down and how people jumped on it. 'How nice would it be, if I could run away?' I thought. 'Run away from school, run away from home and even from this river, and start anew somewhere far away.'

I came to the spot and I opened the sketchbook. The pencil drawing I had started last week looked terrible and I decided to do it over. I realized that the view from the sitting position was a mistake. It did not have the sweeping glance of the scene. It had to be done from the standing position. I had no problem holding the small sketchbook in my hand and drawing standing up. But working on a larger scale, I knew, would be difficult. Harumi and I would need either easels or boards to hang from our necks to hold the paper we would work on.

The center piece was getting done nicely and I moved on to the left sheet. The factory buildings on the other side of the river looked very interesting. I thought they would work well in the picture, but I had some trouble on this side of the river, just a bland green field. 'How can I make it interesting?' I was wondering, when I heard someone calling my name.

I turned around and saw Harumi waving her hand in the distance. There were also four adult figures walking with her toward me. The sight of Harumi's waving hand, at once lifted my spirits. I felt sudden excitement and indescribable joy, and I started to run to her.

"What are you doing here?" I shouted as I reached Harumi.

"We just came for a walk," she said, and held my hand. "It's a beautiful day, isn't it?"

Harumi and I walked hand in hand toward the spot where I was drawing. I showed her what I had done and explained to her that we would have to work standing up, and we would need two easels or boards to work on.

"No problem," Harumi said. "I'll ask my dad to get two easels."

Harumi and I decided to go down to the water. I gave Harumi the sketchbook and two pencils to hold and I rolled down the slope. When I reached the bottom of the slope, I looked up. Harumi was trying to come down slowly by herself, and her mother came running to her side and held her arm. Harumi said something and shrugged off her mother's hand.

I remained on the ground looking at the cloud above. A large mountain of cloud was changing shape slowly showing some valleys and lakes. Harumi came and lay down next to me, and then put her head on my chest.

"I want to hear the sound of your life," said Harumi.

"Your parents are watching us," I said, and tried to get up.

"I don't care!" She held my body so tight that I could not move. I gave up.

The grownups were still standing on top of the dike looking at us.

"How's my heart doing?" I said jokingly.

"It's doing fine," Harumi answered. "It's beating strong, pumping blood throughout your body, keeping you alive."

After a while, Harumi got up. The four people started to come down the slope. Harumi and I walked on the trail down to the water. The water was not as high as last week but flowing rapidly. We stood there and watched. It was always mesmerizing to watch the water of the river flow. The grownups caught up with us and Harumi's mother introduced me to Harumi's aunt and uncle. Harumi and I walked hand in hand, and the four adults were following behind us in awkward silence.

The thick cloud above the three chimneys across the river glowed in vermillion, and the shadow of the flock of birds were cutting across it. From time to time Harumi and I looked at each other and smiled. I felt for a moment that we were together and one in exhilaration and nothing could take away our happiness.

We came to the stone steps leading to top of the dike. Harumi's father came and tried to carry Harumi, but she refused and held my hand tight and climbed up.

"I am tired now," Harumi said, and looked at me. I knew what she wanted, but I was hesitant.

"I'll carry you on my back, Harumi," father said and bent down in front of her.

"No, I want Nobuo to carry me," Harumi said in a strong voice. I was alerted.

"But you are too heavy for Nobuo," her mother said.

I handed my sketchbook and two pencils to Harumi's mother, and went to Harumi. She flushed with a big smile.

'Harumi is not too heavy for me,' I said to myself. 'I must show them, I must carry her like a big person.'

THE KISS

The classroom looked different without Harumi's presence. Sitting in the back of the classroom I was always able to see Harumi, but now I only saw an empty desk instead. The room lost a focal point and it had become a boring mass of chairs, desks and heads.

The first period was the arithmetic test.

"I think I have one hundred!" after the test as soon as Mr. Yoshida left the classroom, Saburo sprang up from the chair and declared.

"Hey, that's great," I said to Saburo.

"Where is Harumi?" Saburo was looking around the classroom. "I want to tell her."

Nobody seemed to know what was happening with Harumi. I wondered if Mr. Yoshida knew anything about her condition. No one seemed to care if she was in the classroom or not except Saburo.

"I don't think she is here," I said and walked away. I didn't want any more questions about Harumi.

After lunch Mr. Yoshida told me that I didn't have to run around the schoolyard anymore, but I had to practice catch with Hiroshi instead. The tournament would start in a few weeks and I needed to get used to Hiroshi's breaking balls. I had to go to the storage room to fetch a catcher's mitt. The storage room was on the ground floor at the other end of the building. Hiroshi was waiting for me on the bench under the cherry trees. He was putting Vaseline on his leather glove.

"Hey, that looks good, new?" I said.

"Yeah, dad got it for me on my birthday." Hiroshi put his face in the glove and took a deep breath. "You want to smell it?"

"Umm... smells so good!" I had never smelled anything like it. It had the distinctive scent of new leather, but there was something else too, a very strong pleasant smell which I could not even describe.

We tossed the ball several times and Hiroshi started to pitch. I did not have too much of a problem with fast balls, but still couldn't catch the curve balls. I asked him to tell me before he threw curve balls. I tried to follow the ball more carefully, tried to pay attention to the speed of the ball and where it turned. After a while I was getting better, at the same time, I was beginning to think it was also the catcher's mitt which was giving me trouble. The mitt was old and worn out, and made of canvas stuffed with straw and cotton. I thought I should use my own pigskin glove instead.

The bell rang. Hiroshi walked with me to the storage room to return the mitt.

"I still feel bad about the last game," said Hiroshi, as we were walking back to the classroom. "I let everyone down..."

"Listen, Hiroshi," I cut him off. "If I didn't make an error, the game could have been a tie even with your error. We should just enjoy playing ball without getting hung up on winning or losing so much."

Hiroshi shrugged his shoulders, and smiled.

The last period was the science test. Unlike after the arithmetic test, Saburo was not exuberant.

"How did you do?" I asked him.

"Okay, I guess," said Saburo shaking his head.

Because of the two tests we did not have homework but I remained in the classroom after the dismissal. I was standing by the window wondering what to do. I didn't want to go home.

"Aren't you going home?" It was Saburo.

"You are still here," I said.

Saburo said he had something to tell me. So we decided to go to the river. It was an unusually warm day, almost like summer.

"I smell summer coming." As soon as we climbed up the dike, I took a deep breath. I remembered that was exactly what Harumi said a few weeks ago.

"Today summer, tomorrow you will smell winter," said Saburo. We were having strange weather these days, one day cold and next day very warm.

"We are moving," as we were sitting down on the slope Saburo said.

"What?" I said and looked at him. He was smiling.

"Yup, moving out of the village." I could see Saburo was excited. "We are moving to Osaka."

"When?" It was too sudden and I couldn't believe it. Although I knew it was great for Saburo and his family to be able to move out of the village, I was not ready to hear it especially now that Harumi was going to have the operation in a few days.

"My dad will be leaving in a few weeks," Saburo said. "The rest of us will stay until the end of the school term, and we will move in August."

I was kind of relieved to know that at least he would be here until summer. I never thought of Saburo as anything but a kid who happened to be placed next to me in the classroom. I had not realized until then that Saburo had become a real good friend and such an important part of my school life. Saburo told me that he received a large sum of the reward money from the bank, and his parents and Kyoko's mother split it, and at the same time Saburo's father got a job at the Korean organization in Osaka to run the newly created Korean youth program. Kyoko and her mother were moving with them too. It was indeed great news.

"Congrats! I am very happy for you," I said, and I meant it with all my heart.

That night, a small black swirl started in the corner of the room I was sleeping in. It was growing bigger and spinning faster and faster. I was frightened and tried to get up, but my body was tied to the ground and I could not move. The swirl became big, and it was hovering over my face and about to swallow me up. I screamed and screamed.

"Nobuo, Nobuo.....wake up." I heard my mother's voice in the distance. I wiggled my body to free myself. Mother pulled me up from the ground.

I awoke in mother's arms, but the black swirl kept spinning in my eyes. Mother tried to put me on the futon and told me to go back to sleep, but I was clinging to her. I was too afraid to go to sleep. I kept my eyes wide open until the image of the swirl faded away.

"Nobuo, wake up, you are late for school." My mother woke me up in the morning. I had a headache and felt like the energy had been drained out of my body. I did not want to go to school, but I had no choice.

I knew Harumi was not coming to school, but I waited at the corner for a while.

"Your wife is late today," those same four kids shouted at me as they were running past. It made me angry, but I didn't have the energy to go after them. 'I know who they are,' I thought. 'I could find them any time I want.'

Time passed slowly in the class. I didn't even open the book I brought from home. I didn't feel like reading or doing anything. I could not stop thinking about Harumi.

I played catch with Hiroshi during the lunch break. I brought my own glove from home, and I did much better. I was not afraid of Hiroshi's breaking balls anymore.

We had some homework but I did not want to stay after school with Saburo and others. On the way home I took a detour and went past Harumi's house three times. There was no sign of anyone in the house. I thought that they must still be at the hospital. I came home feeling exhausted.

I had been thinking of *love*, the concept Harumi was so hung up on. After dinner I decided to look it up and took out a big dictionary from my father's bookshelf.

There were two words for *love* in Japanese, *koi* and *ai*. Those two could be combined and pronounced *ren-ai*. According to the dictionary, *koi* meant longing and caring between man and woman. The word *ai* had a wider meaning; caring and consideration for human and other living things, caring between parents and children and between siblings, and also it included the definition of *koi*. The word *ren-ai* represented feeling of *koi* and *ai* between man and woman, and the attitudes and actions based on that feeling. I tried to digest what the dictionary said, and at the same time I thought about the feeling I had for Harumi. I came to the conclusion that I did love her.

Around nine o'clock, mother took out the futons and laid them on the tatami floor preparing for the night. I did not want to go to sleep because the black swirl remained vividly in my memory and I was scared.

All five of us children slept on three futons in the six tatami room. My two sisters shared one futon, and two brothers shared another. I had my own futon because I was big and dangerous; I kicked everyone and everything around me during my sleep. Father and mother slept in the next room which had four and a half tatami. During the day all futons were put away in the closets, and our parents' bedroom became the family room and dining room with the folding table being placed in the center.

As I was reluctantly changing to nightwear, there was a knock on the front door. The entryway was connected to the two tatami room next to the room where we slept, separated by the fusuma screens.

"Who could it be this late?" My mother went to answer the door mumbling.

"I am sorry to disturb you at this late hour." I recognized the voice immediately; it was Harumi's mother.

My heart started pounding rapidly. 'Something must have happened to Harumi.' I was so worried that I was about to cry.

"My daughter, Harumi will be going to the hospital tomorrow. She'll be having an operation on Thursday, and it's terribly selfish of her, but she wants to talk to your son..." I ripped my nightwear off and changed to my day clothes and opened the fusuma screen before Harumi's mother finished her sentence.

"It wouldn't take long; I will bring him back as soon...." I was out of the door but she was still bowing and telling my mother all kinds of nonsense. How I wished she would just shut up and get out of here.

My mother was sitting on the floor and looked stunned, and just bowed to Harumi's mother without a word. I had to go back in, and literally pushed Harumi's mother out of the entryway.

"I am so sorry, Nobuo." Now it was my turn to be apologized to. "You must've been asleep...." I tried to walk with her, pretending that I was listening to what she was saying, but I could not take it any longer, so I started to run.

I went through the side door at the gate, and ran up to the front door.

Before I reached it, the sliding door was opened from inside. I faced Harumi standing there.

"Nobuo, thank you....." Harumi came down on the stone and grabbed my hands. "I had to see you."

I was short of breath and too excited and couldn't say anything. I saw Harumi's father standing in the hallway, and I managed to bow to him. He just smiled at me and went away. Harumi led me to her room, and I heard Harumi's mother opening the door and coming into the house.

"I wanted to see you so bad," Harumi said. "I was thinking about you all day."

"I wanted to see you too." I was still breathing heavily.

"Wait a sec, I'll get you some water." Harumi went out of the room. I sat on the bed.

Harumi came back with a glass of water, and I gulped it down in one shot.

"So good to see you," I said. "I was thinking of you all day too."

Harumi took the glass out of my hand and put it on the small table. She sat next to me, held my hand and put her head on my shoulder. We stayed like that for some time without a word.

"I wanted to give you something," said Harumi and stood up and went to her desk. She brought back a bunch of stuff and put them on the bed.

"This is the Andersen book, A *Picture-Book Without Pictures*." She handed me a small paperback, and then a large square book. "This is your favorite book of Klee's paintings."

"Why are you giving me these?" I didn't like it. I sensed that she was saying goodbye to me. "You are not going away for good, are you?"

"No, not at all." Harumi looked surprised by my question. "I don't know how long I will stay in the hospital, so I just want you to keep these for me until I come home. I thought you would enjoy them."

"All right then," I said. "Can I come and see you in the hospital?

"You will be the first person I want to see after the operation." I saw the sweetest smile I've ever seen on her face.

She handed me another book, this one was shiny red, leather bound and it had a snap on belt on it.

"This is a notebook of my poetry; I want you to read it sometime." I tried to open the snap, but she put her hands on my arm and stopped me. "Not now please, sometime later."

"I want to tell you something," I said looking at her eyes. "You asked me once if I loved you and I answered I didn't know." It took a lot of courage for me to say this much. Harumi was staring back at me and waiting. "I looked it up in the dictionary and now I know that I love you."

Harumi started to laugh with her mouth open. I felt so embarrassed that I wanted to run away.

"I am sorry I laughed," Harumi stopped laughing and said, "Thank you, and I love you too, it's just.....I didn't need to look it up though."

This time I laughed and Harumi was smiling.

"Now, you must kiss me." Harumi stopped smiling and became serious. "Do you know how to kiss?"

"No, I don't." I was taken aback by this.

"Then, close your eyes," Harumi ordered and I closed my eyes as told.

I felt something soft and warm pressed on my lips. It was just a split second and then it was gone. Harumi took a deep breath.

"Now, I am ready for tomorrow," said Harumi with a big smile.

Harumi's mother was taking me home. Harumi came outside at the door and was waving her hand until I reached the gate to the street.

"Thank you so much for coming," her mother started again. "I am sorry I had to wake you up."

"Thank you for coming to get me, I was very happy to see Harumi."
I tried to shut her up. "Can I come and see Harumi in the hospital?"

"Of course, as soon as the doctor says all right, I will take you there."

We were at the front door of our house, and I asked her to leave so that my mother wouldn't have to get up. She agreed and left quietly. I didn't want to hear their long greetings again. My mother was up and waiting for me.

"Harumi's mother left because she didn't want to disturb you in case you were asleep," I said to my mother.

"That's fine, please go to sleep," mother said. "It's getting very late."

She waited for me to change my clothes and slip onto the futon, and then she turned the light off. I was glad that she didn't question me about anything.

I closed my eyes and I touched my lips with my fingertips. I vividly recalled the soft and warm touch of Harumi's lips, which made me shiver.

I saw the black swirl again in the corner of the room. I stared at it, and said to myself that I wasn't afraid. It stayed in the corner for a while and disappeared.

DEATH

It had been an uneventful day in school. There was a social studies test of simple geography at the end of the day. After collecting the test sheets from the kids, Mr. Yoshida made an announcement.

"I have sad news to report, Harumi died in the hospital this morning. There will be a funeral at her parents' house at eleven o'clock tomorrow. Each of you must bring a condolence gift of ten yen to school."

Just like that. It was a very simple and clear announcement but I had trouble comprehending the message. 'Harumi is dead? Funeral? A condolence gift?' Those words didn't really sink in; they were just words, carrying no meaning or reality. The whole classroom fell into an eerie silence. 'Where am I anyway? What am I doing here?' I was disoriented.

Saburo looked at me with tears in his eyes, and it hit me. I stood up and hung the backpack on my shoulder and walked up to the front, went past Mr. Yoshida to the door.

"Nobuo, where are you going?" Mr. Yoshida tried to grab my arm, but I shook him off and ran. I ran through the hallways, ran down the staircase and ran out the door to the street. When I ran up the slope to the top of the dike, tears started to rush down on my cheeks. I went a few steps down the slope toward the river and sat down on the grass.

"How could it be possible?" I said to myself out loud. I saw her two nights ago. She was talking to me, she held my hand and kissed me. I touched my lips and I was still able to feel Harumi's soft and warm lips. I didn't get it. I didn't understand what had been happening here. "Harumi is dead? I cannot see her anymore?" Then, my mind went blank.

I heard a whistle blow and saw a long freight train crossing the bridge. I saw the river flowing quietly. I felt an excruciating pain in my heart. 'I am alive..., and Harumi is gone!' It finally became a reality, and I screamed my guts out, and cried, cried and cried....

I felt some weight on my shoulder and I looked up. Mr. Yoshida was sitting next to me gently putting his arm around my shoulders. I tried to stop crying, but couldn't. As we were, without a word, we remained there for a long time. Tears dried out. Suddenly I felt cold and started shivering.

"Let's go home," Mr. Yoshida squeezed my shoulder and said. "I'll take you home."

The path on the dike we were walking on was the same path I had walked on carrying Harumi on my back just a few days ago. The sky, the river and the green field, they all looked the same as always as if nothing had happened. How could it be possible that everything surrounding us stayed indifferent to Harumi's death? Would everything remain the same and the world would go on forever even if I died? I looked up to Mr. Yoshida's face. He too didn't look any different. Though I appreciated his silence, I wondered and wanted to know what he was feeling, what he was thinking, and why he was walking me home. We came to the stone steps which led to the street below.

"I can go home now, you don't need to come with me," I said to Mr. Yoshida looking straight at his face.

"I want to see you home," Mr. Yoshida said with a gentle smile.

'How can he smile at me?' I thought. 'Harumi is dead and he is smiling at me, something's wrong here!'

My mother was outside in the front garden. She seemed to be tending the flowers, but I could tell she was waiting for me. She must have known about Harumi's death.

"Big brother is home!" my youngest brother, Tomo screamed. My brothers were playing with bamboo swords. "Let's play sword fighting." Both of them came running to me.

I ignored them and opened the door and went inside. Mother and Mr. Yoshida started the greeting ritual. I ripped my backpack off my shoulder and threw it on the tatami floor, and looked for my small sketchbook.

'Harumi promised me, she would come back from the hospital and we would work on the panorama painting together.' Now, I was angry. 'She lied!' I was so mad that my eyes started to well up. I found three drawings I had made for the painting and lined them up on the floor. I looked at them for a few seconds, and then ripped them into little pieces one by one. I brought the large drawing pad and ripped every drawing and watercolor into pieces.

I opened the closet where the futon mattresses were stored and found some room in the corner. I crawled into it and closed the fusuma screen. I was in complete darkness and finally I felt safe. 'I should stay here forever, never to go out in the open again.' I thought. 'In here, I don't have to see anyone, I don't have to talk to anyone.' I was angry, angry at Harumi, angry at everyone and everything, at the same time I was having pain in my heart with such a deep sadness, a sadness which I never felt before.

A commotion woke me up. For a moment I forgot where I was. It sounded like everyone was looking for me. I opened the fusuma door.

"He is here, he is here!" Tomo cried out and came face to face with me.

"Big brother is in the closet."

My father sat next to me at the dinner table.

"I heard your friend died," when we finished eating and having tea, he spoke to me. "It must have been a shock to you. You must be strong, and remember, life is for the living."

I didn't want to talk to him so I didn't say anything, but he made me angry.

'What does it mean *life is for the living?*' I wanted to scream at him. 'What about Harumi, we should all forget about her?'

The black swirl started small in the corner. I tried to fight it, kept telling myself that I was not afraid. Slowly it was growing bigger. It had an opening in the center like a mouth and the inside was dark red. As it was spinning the mouth was repeating the same movement; opening wide quickly and closing slowly. All of a sudden the fear struck me like thunder, and the swirl exploded, and the red mouth was swallowing me up. I screamed.

"Nobuo, wake up," I heard my mother calling, I tried to reach out to her, but I could not move. I kept screaming. I was slapped on my cheek and awoke, but the swirl was still in front of me spinning fast.

"It's there, the black swirl!" I yelled and pointed my finger at the swirl. "It's going to swallow me!"

"You are having a nightmare." I recognized my father's voice. "There's nothing there."

"It's right there, can't you see?" How could they not see it? It was right in front of us. I kept pointing my finger at it.

Mother brought a glass of water for me. I took a sip but I had trouble swallowing it and spilled the water on my nightwear. Then I realized that my whole body was wet from sweating. Mother wiped my body with a thin cotton towel and changed me into a summer kimono.

The black swirl was gone, but I had a very difficult time going back to sleep. I kept tossing and turning and I was frustrated and exhausted.

I did not want to go to school in the morning, so I lied to my mother telling her that the morning classes were cancelled because of the funeral. She believed me. My sisters had left the house already and mother was taking my brothers out of the alleyway to the street to send them off to school. Meanwhile, I found a small cotton bag in the kitchen and picked up the piggybank and went to the front garden. The piggybank was surprisingly heavy and I had to hold it with two hands against my chest. I put the piggybank on the flat stone imbedded in the ground near the bench on the side of the house, and went around the garden to look for another stone. I found one under the fence of the next property. I brought it back to the side of the house and smashed the piggybank in one stroke. Coins and bills were scattered around, I picked them up and stuffed them into the cotton bag. I took the school stuff out of my backpack and put the cotton bag in it. Then I went to the kitchen and found two sweet breads and some rice crackers, and filled a canteen with water, and put them all in the backpack. I waited till eleven o'clock.

Mother was in the garden cutting some flowers. I said good bye to her, and she waved at me.

From the corner, I could see a bunch of people gathered around Harumi's house. Kids from my class were already there. Those kids who did not care whether Harumi was in the class or not were lining up in front of the house. Those girls who were jealous of Harumi because they thought she was favored by teachers were there. 'They were there for what?' I wondered. 'Are they there to see Harumi's corpse, or are they there only because Mr. Yoshida dragged them down there?'

I joined my classmates on the line. There was a small table where an elderly lady was sitting, collecting condolence gifts. It was the Japanese custom that you brought money to a funeral as a condolence gift. There was a pile of envelopes on the table and kids were putting a ten yen coins in the ceramic bowl. I took my backpack off my shoulder and took out the cotton bag. When it came to my turn I emptied the bag into the ceramic bowl, threw the bag on the ground and turned around. Some coins fell out of the bowl and rolled onto the table and to the ground. The elderly lady looked stunned and tried to say something, but I was already going out the gate. I never wanted to see Harumi's corpse, I didn't want to listen to the Buddhist monk mumbling, and I didn't want to light the incense stick. This whole ceremony had nothing to do with Harumi and seemed totally absurd. I could not even imagine myself participating in it. I heard Mr. Yoshida calling my name, so I ran. I ran to the river.

I ran up to the top of the dike and stopped. I felt very tired, and for a moment I thought I would collapse right then and there. I took a deep breath and sat on the grass. I closed my eyes and waited for the energy to come back to my body. After a while I managed to get up and started to walk.

'I must get to the bridge before dark, and then I will be all right.' I thought. I did not have a clear idea how far the bridge was, or how long it would take to get there by walking.

I heard kids' voices down below, talking, screaming and laughing. I was passing by the school. It must have been lunch break; I saw many kids playing in the schoolyard. Everything seemed to be normal, nothing had changed. I was astonished to know how insignificant Harumi's death was to the world. Then, I realized that my existence, my life was equally insignificant to the world. It was really funny to me because lately I was beginning to think that the whole world was revolving around me. I was beginning to think, maybe I was the center of the universe; without me the world would not function properly. How wrong could I have been! How stupid of me to think that I was so important.

I was getting hungry, but I made sure I walked far enough from the school before I sat down. I ate two sweet breads stuffed with red beans and had some water. I became so sleepy and lay down.

I had no idea how long I slept or what time it was when I woke up. The sun was still up and it was warm. I stood up and stretched myself. There was no reason to carry the backpack anymore, so I took out the canteen and hung it from my shoulder and put the rice crackers in my pants pocket. I left the backpack right there and resumed the trekking. I saw the long freight train crossing over the bridge. The bridge did not look any closer than it did from where I had started, but I was not discouraged. I thought I had plenty of time to get there.

I was trying not to think about Harumi but it was difficult. Everywhere I looked the images of Harumi appeared superimposed, smiling face, her lying with long black hair spread on the grass. I even heard her voice singing *Raining Moon*.

'Did she know she was going to die?' I could not help wondering. 'Is that why she gave me those books?' I thought for a moment that I should have brought those books with me, but quickly changed my mind. I did not need anything to remind me of Harumi's death. Harumi promised me a lot of things; she promised that she would come back and work on the panorama painting with me; she promised that she would go to the museum with me to look at my work if it were exhibited, she said she would teach me how to swim in the summer... If she had known that she was not coming back, how could she promise all those things? Maybe she didn't know; maybe she was hopeful that the operation would be successful and she would get better. My thoughts were racing all over and there was no solution.

All of a sudden, I noticed that the sun disappeared and the sky was getting darker, also the air was getting cooler. I saw a big vertical sign for the *Tama River Amusement Park*, where my father had taken my brothers and me a few times. The bridge looked not too far. I was very thirsty and hungry. I sat on the slope and drank the remaining water in the canteen and threw away the canteen. The rice crackers were not my favorite but they tasted so good, I ate them all.

I was right under the bridge. The bridge looked so pretty from afar but it looked quite different from close up. It was a huge rusty iron structure, and looked rather scary. I heard people saying that the train slowed down just before the bridge and you could hop on the train, but the bridge was hovering over the dike and I did not see how I could even go near the track. After looking around for some time, I went down the slope on the opposite side of the river and climbed another slope covered with gravel. There was a very narrow path at the top, and I followed it. There they were, railroad tracks. I found the mound of gravel near the track and sat down. It was getting dark. I looked around and saw the never ending stretch of the railroad, but I was attacked by sudden exhaustion; all my strength, energy and will power drained out of me. I felt sad, lonely and hopeless. I waited for a long time but the train never came. It was completely dark now and getting cold and I was very uncomfortable sitting on the gravel. I stood up and walked on the path trying to go back to the dike of the river. On the slope I slipped and fell on my side. I went down with a bunch of gravel to the bottom. I hit my head and was bleeding on my left arm. I crawled up the grassy slope and reached the top of the dike. I went several steps down on the river side of the slope and collapsed.

At first I thought I was dreaming. I thought that I heard Harumi calling my name and she was standing in front of me. I tried to reach out but no one was there. I saw the big and bright moon looking down on me.

"Nobuo-chan!" I heard it clearly and stood up.

"He is here!" It was a woman's voice. "I found him!"

She ran to me with open arms and tried to hold me, but I was pushed down and fell on the ground and she came down with me.

"Nobuo-chan, so good to have found you." The woman was holding me tight and crying. Her tears were dropping all over my face. I started to cry also.

"We found him!" a man's voice called out. "He is all right."

Two men helped us get up. The woman was still holding me and crying. It was Harumi's mother. The two men were, I recognized, Harumi's father and Mr. Yoshida. Mr. Yoshida was carrying my backpack and canteen. Two other men were coming up the slope from the river side. One was my father and the other was my cousin who lived next door. Harumi's mother finally let go of me.

"Oh, my!" she looked at my left arm and shrieked, "You are bleeding." She took out a handkerchief from her skirt pocket and wet it in her mouth and cleaned the wound. Tears were coming out of her eyes again.

"Let me carry you on my back." My father came and lowered himself. I climbed onto his back and clung to his neck. Father's warmth was transferring to my body and I felt relaxed and peaceful.

Mother prepared a bath and was waiting for us at home. She did not seem to have been worried so much. She smiled wide when she saw me. She cleaned up the wound on my arm with alcohol and put some ointment on it, and then bandaged it up. She stripped my clothes off and put me in the bathtub.

"I knew you'd be all right," she muttered as she was putting a summer kimono on me.

ZEN TEMPLE

Surprisingly I had a good night's sleep with no nightmares; the black swirl didn't show up. It was Saturday but I decided not to go to school. I pretended that I was asleep until my sisters and brothers left. Mother did not try to wake me. I was thinking about yesterday. I tried to run away from here and failed miserably. I did not expect anyone to come looking for me. Mr. Yoshida and Harumi's parents were there looking for me, which was a surprise. I did not think anyone would care if I was around or not. Was I happy that they came and found me? Not really; quite honestly I didn't care. I didn't think about what would have happened if they did not find me. I thought whatever would have happened would've been all right with me. I thought that I should try again sometime, but next time I would have to have a better plan.

"Are you still asleep?" said mother putting her palm on my forehead. She came back from the street where she had seen my brothers off to school. "You should get up and have breakfast."

Mother was extremely gentle with me which was very unusual. 'Is it because of yesterday?' I wondered. 'But why?' I didn't quite understand.

Until I started to eat I didn't realize how hungry I was. I ate two bowls of rice with fermented soybean called *natto*, some seaweed, a bowl of miso-soup, and a fried egg. After I finished eating, I crawled into the closet and squeezed myself between futon mattresses. My brain was empty; I could not think. I was getting squashed by the heavy helplessness.

"I see you." The fusuma door was opened and Tomo stuck his face in the closet. I must have fallen asleep. My brothers were already back from school. "Can I come in too?"

"No, Tomo," mother yelled. "Lunch is ready. Nobuo, you cannot go in there, your brothers will copy you."

When I finished eating, Tomo and my younger brother Isao were waiting, and attacked me from behind; they wanted to play wrestling. I pushed them aside so hard that Tomo fell on his face onto the tatami mat and Isao landed on him. Tomo began to cry.

"Nobuo, that was not nice!" mother came over and screamed at me. "Go outside and play."

I went outside but didn't want to go anywhere. I went around to the side of the house and sat on the bench. The pieces of the crushed ceramic piggybank were still scattered around the flat stone. The old pink-colored piggybank was all bits and pieces now, but there were some recognizable shapes like the nose, ears and tail. I went to the shed at the corner of the garden and got a broom and a trash pan. As I was sweeping those pieces into the trash pan I felt a little sad. It wasn't that I had any regret for what I had done yesterday, but looking at the broken pieces I missed my old piggy.

"You want to play sword fight?" Isao came out and stood in front of me and said. Tomo was right behind him.

"No, I don't want to play with you, go away," I said with an angry voice. They did not go away; instead they sat next to me on the bench. I decided to ignore them.

My sisters came home. They had piano lessons somewhere after school on Saturdays. My eldest sister, Michiko came and looked at us and laughed.

"What are you guys doing, all lined up on the bench?"

"Nobuo doesn't want to play with us," Tomo said.

"Then come with me, I'll show you something," said Michiko. Isao and Tomo jumped off the bench and followed her.

Mother turned the light off, and soon my brothers were sound asleep, but I was not sleepy. Father was not home yet and both of my sisters were in the next room talking with mother. I had my eyes open and lay still on the futon, and waited. I had a strong feeling that the black swirl was going to appear. The bell on the clock on the wall chimed ten times and soon afterward father came home. I kept lying still with my eyes open. My sisters came into the room and settled onto their futon. I heard father and mother talking for a while, but soon the whole house was quiet. I closed my eyes but could not fall asleep. The clock's bell chimed eleven times. I could not keep still any longer, so I sat up and looked around. It was dark and I could not see anything; still I kept my eyes open as wide as I could. I became restless and I wanted to scream but managed to control myself. After for a while I was exhausted and lay down.

I could not wake up in the morning. Mother came and tried to wake me three times. Finally I got off the futon. Everyone else was up and had already finished their breakfast. I was so tired and did not have much appetite.

"Are you going to work on a painting or drawing today?" father asked me after breakfast, when I was just sitting around and thinking of going into the closet to hide.

"No, I don't want to do that kind of stuff anymore," I said.

"Why?" he sat in front of me on the tatami floor and asked. I thought it was kind of strange because he hardly ever talked to me. He said only necessary things and occasionally a few words which meant something, but we never really communicated. He was a quiet and detached man who did not have real passion for anything, I thought. To me, my mother and father seemed totally opposite. My mother was passionate, excitable and always doing something. I did not have much respect for my father.

"It doesn't interest me anymore," I said. "I just don't feel like doing it."

"If you are not doing anything, I want to take you somewhere today," he said and stood up. "Come, get ready."

"Take me to where?" I said and lay down on the tatami. "I don't want to go anywhere."

"Come on, you might find it interesting." He grabbed my arm, and pulled me up.

We took a local train to Shibuya and changed to another train, and after several stops we got off. We walked about ten minutes on the paved street and turned onto a dirt road and climbed up a gentle hill for a short while. There were two low stone columns at the end of the road with no gates or fences, which was the entryway to an old temple building.

As soon as my father opened the wood framed glass sliding door a man came to answer. He had a shaved head and was wearing a typical monk costume; white kimono top and black skirt like pants called *hakama*. They bowed to each other and said some greetings. They seemed to know each other well. Father told me the monk was the master of this temple and his name was Shouzen Sato, and people called him Monk Shouzen.

"Oh, good looking boy," said the monk with a big smile as my father introduced me as his oldest son. "How old are you?"

"I will be twelve in a few days," I said.

"Is that right?" The monk looked surprised. "You are big for your age. I have a fifteen years old nephew here; he is no bigger than you. You will meet him later."

We took our shoes off and entered the hall, and the monk led us to a large room with a wood floor. He brought out two thin futon mats of about thirty inches square and placed them a few feet apart on the floor. Father sat on one of the futon mats and he crossed his legs in a ceremonial fashion.

"You are going to practice Zen meditation," said the monk, and told me to sit like my father. I sat on the mat and crossed my legs. Then the monk corrected me by placing my left foot on my right thigh.

"Relax your shoulders, keep your back straight and pull your chin in," he demanded, placed my left hand on my right palm, and made the tips of my thumbs meet. Then he pointed to the floor about three feet ahead of me.

"Your eyes should be open half way and they should focus on this spot; try not to think about anything. I will be back in a half hour," he said and walked away.

I thought it was the most ridiculous thing I had been asked to do in my whole life. First of all I was forced to sit in the most uncomfortable position, then there was nothing to keep my focus on the floor, and not to think about anything for half an hour was not possible. I looked at my father. He was motionless as a statue. It was the longest thirty minutes of my life.

"Good, very good, you kept your posture somewhat," the monk came back and said to me. "At least you didn't run away. Ha ha...," He started to laugh.

'Gee, I should have,' I thought. 'I didn't know I had a choice."

My father untangled his legs and sat straight and bowed to the monk.

I had trouble freeing my right leg. We were led to a smaller but spacious room overlooking a Japanese garden. Unlike all the other settings, this room looked and even smelled new with green tatami mats and polished wood columns. The garden too looked manicured and beautifully maintained. We sat on the floor near the black lacquered table. The monk excused himself and left the room.

"Nice place, ha?" Father was smiling. I didn't respond. "So peaceful, isn't it amazing, a place like this in the middle of Tokyo?"

"I hate this place," I said. "Let's go home." I was angry at him. He was still smiling which made me angrier.

"You haven't seen the whole place yet." Father was looking at the garden. "There is a large pond in the back."

"Who cares? I don't want to see anything," I said and stood up. "Let's go!"

The monk was coming back carrying a tray with a large glass bowl on it. There were thin white noodles in the water in the glass bowl. A boy with a bald head but wearing regular pants and shirt was following him, carrying another tray full of dishes and small bowls. The monk put the glass bowl and dishes on the table, and introduced me to the boy who was his nephew. His name was Tadashi.

The noodles are called *soh-men*, it was rather a very simple summer dish and one of my favorite ways to eat noodles, so I sat down. There was a large dish full of assorted pickled vegetables; white cabbage, cucumbers, eggplant, turnips and radish. The monk told us proudly that those were all harvested from his vegetable garden, and he had pickled them himself. It turned out to be a good lunch and I really enjoyed it.

"Tadashi, you show Nobuo around," after we had all finished eating the monk told the boy. We got up and I followed Tadashi.

"Let's get out of here," as soon as we were alone in the hallway, Tadashi said and headed to the entrance. We went behind the building and Tadashi took a path which lead straight into the woods. We walked in the woods for a few minutes and suddenly we were in a clearing. There was a large wild looking pond.

"There are a lot of crawfish in there," Tadashi said. "Some big carp too."

"Can you fish here?" I asked.

"Monk Shouzen doesn't allow anyone to fish carp, but I used to catch crawfish a lot," Tadashi said as we were walking by the water. There were some tall weeds growing out of the water here and there.

"How do you catch crawfish?" I had never seen crawfish and I became curious.

"It's simple; tie a string to a piece of dried squid, and throw it in the water," said Tadashi. "The greedy crawfish grabs the squid and won't let it go even after it gets brought out of the water."

"Sounds like fun, can I try it?" I was getting excited.

"Not today, but come back sometime, I will show you."

"Who taught you that?" I asked.

"Monk Shouzen," said Tadashi as he turned to the path going away from the water to higher ground. "He showed me a lot of interesting stuff to keep me here at the beginning."

"Do you live here?" I thought he was just visiting his uncle for a day or something. "How did you wind up here?"

"Did Monk Shouzen let you sit?" instead of answering my question he turned to me and asked. I nodded. "Did you stay?" I nodded again. "For whole half hour?" I nodded. "That's great, amazing! You know, he did that to me on the first day when I came here too. There were two college guys besides me. I ran away and hid in the woods until dark."

"What happened then?" I said thinking about myself of two days ago.

"He left the lights on everywhere and waited for me to come back with dinner ready."

"Didn't he come out to look for you?"

"No, he did not. I guess he knew I would be back," he said with a smile.

We came to a small shack standing on a stone foundation. Tadashi opened the wooden door. The inside looked roomier than it appeared from outside. There was no window but a light bulb was suspended from the ceiling in the middle of the room. A guitar was placed against the wall and a big poster of a foreigner with a cowboy hat was pinned above it. There was a platform at the opposite end of the room, and a narrow bench was on the right side of the room.

"This is my hideout," said Tadashi as he jumped onto the platform. "This used to be a storage room, full of junk like old furniture, books, tools and stuff. Monk Shouzen let me clean it all out last summer, and allowed me to use it as my playhouse."

"Why do you live in the temple; don't you have parents?" I said and sat on the bench.

"Of course I have parents," Tadashi said and looked at me. I knew he was wondering whether he should answer my question or not.

"When did you come here?" I changed my question.

"About four years ago," Tadashi answered but he was still hesitant to tell me the whole story. After a few minutes of silence he said. "Okay, I'll tell you."

The temple had been owned and operated by the Sato family for hundreds of years. When Tadashi's grandfather passed away, Monk Shouzen took over the reign because he was the eldest son. He had a brother, who was Tadashi's father, and two sisters. Monk Shouzen was married, but had no children while Tadashi's parents had two sons and a daughter. Tadashi was the second son and the youngest child. Five years ago Monk Shouzen's wife died. Since Monk Shouzen had no intention of getting married again, the Sato family had to decide the heir to the temple. There was a meeting of all the relatives of Monk Shouzen, and they picked Tadashi as heir apparent mainly because he was the son of Monk Shouzen's only brother, and he was the second son. Customarily, the oldest son was to remain with his own family no matter what and carry on the family name.

"It's all a family business you know," Tadashi said. "This has little to do with religion."

"Are you okay with that?" I said. "Were you happy when they picked you?"

"No way, I wasn't happy at all," said Tadashi and jumped off the platform and grabbed the guitar. "I hated anything and everything about this place. I missed my family especially my brother and my friends."

"Then, why are you still here?" I really wondered. I thought that I would never stay if I hated it that much.

"As time went by I began to understand the situation and more and more I became fond of Monk Shouzen. He is actually a very good man and really believes in Zen Buddhism." Tadashi plucked a few notes on the guitar. "He teaches Japanese at the local middle school as a substitute teacher also. He kept telling me: 'You were chosen, accept the challenge and work on it.' Now I have been thinking he may be right."

'This kid has been brainwashed,' I thought but did not say anything.

"Do you know Hank Williams?" said Tadashi and started to sing while he strummed his guitar. It was a somewhat familiar tune and he was singing in English. Our radio was always tuned to the classical music station, but my cousin who lived next door to us often listened to this kind of music.

"Who's that?" I waited for him to finish singing and asked.

"He is the greatest country singer in America. That's him." He pointed his finger at the poster on the wall. "I have a friend in school whose father works at the American Army base. He gave me that. He has some records too."

"You have your own radio?" I noticed a small radio by the back wall on the platform. "You are lucky; you have a hideout like this, and your own radio and guitar. When I want to hide I crawl into the futon closet."

"Ha, ha, ha..." Tadashi laughed. "Yeah, I have quite a bit of freedom here. We made a kind of deal, Monk Shouzen and I, that as long as I keep up with the training to be a monk I can do anything I want."

"What kind of training do you do?" I was curious.

"You see, there are nine people living in the temple right now, including three college students who are renting rooms here. We all get up at five o'clock in the morning and clean the place, have breakfast and meditate for forty five minutes before we start the day. I am sent to the temple in Kyoto every summer for ten days for training also."

I thought it was pretty crazy. I could not imagine myself getting up at five o'clock and meditating for forty five minutes every morning.

"Do you want to know what I listen to on the radio?" said Tadashi and turned the radio on. There was male voice speaking English. "This is FEN; Far East Network, American Army station. You could listen to current hit music in America, you know. It helps my English too. Those English teachers in school, they cannot speak the language at all; sometimes they can't even pronounce some words correctly. I bet I have better pronunciation ability than most of them, thanks to FEN."

"That's cool; I wish I had my own radio. I would do exactly the same as you," I said. I wanted to learn English. My mother was teaching me from time to time how to say things in English, but I wanted to learn the language correctly.

Monk Shouzen and my father were walking toward us.

"Time to go, I guess," Tadashi said. "Come again sometime, you will find me here on Sunday afternoons."

My father and I were on the train heading home.

"Did you have fun with Tadashi? father asked me.

"Yes, I did," I answered. It was refreshing to meet someone so different from kids I knew in school.

"I knew you two would get along," father said.

BIRTHDAY

Wednesday, June 2nd, it was my birthday. I became twelve years old.

Even though there was a law since 1902, to use one's birthday in order to calculate one's age in Japan, the whole society kept using the calendar year. The calendar year was based on the Buddhists' belief that life begins when a baby is conceived, so the time a baby spends in the mother's womb is counted as a year. Therefore, the moment a baby is born he or she is already one year old. Then on January 1st, everyone automatically gains one year. If you were born on December 31st, the next day you would become two years old. New Year's Day is treated like everyone's birthday. This tradition began to change four years ago in 1950, when citizens were encouraged to follow the existing law of 1902.

But when I turned twelve, still birthdays did not mean much and were not celebrated.

I woke up late, and took time to finish breakfast. I did not want to go to school. School reminded me of Harumi and her absence was unbearable. By the time I reached school the morning assembly was over and the kids were settled in the classrooms. For the past three days I had avoided the assembly this way. I thought I was lucky on Monday and Tuesday because Mr. Yoshida was not in the classroom when I came in, but I was a little too late this morning.

"I am sorry I am late," I said as I was walking into the classroom.

"You have been late every day this week," Mr. Yoshida said. "You must come on time."

"Yes sir," I said and wondered, 'How did he know? Why didn't he say anything if he knew?' I was standing in front of him waiting for some kind of punishment.

"Go to your desk," Mr. Yoshida said.

"I am giving you a surprise test this morning." Before I even sat down, Mr. Yoshida was handing papers out to the class. Kids groaned.

Twenty *Kanji* was listed on the paper. We were supposed to write the pronunciation and definition of each *Kanji* and a short sentence using each one. I looked at every *Kanji* carefully; I knew them all. It was an easy test but I didn't feel like writing answers. I thought about writing a short story using all twenty *Kanji* on the back of the test paper but I gave up the idea because I did not think I could incorporate four or five of them into a story. I signed my name on the front and decided that I would just leave the answers blank. I did not think about the consequences, I didn't care. Harumi's absence was killing me and I could not stop thinking about her. I knew that she had died and I would not see her ever again but still could not fully understand and accept her death.

The bell rang and it was the end of the period. Mr. Yoshida collected the test sheets and left the room. Saburo saw my blank paper and looked astonished. He turned to me with his mouth open, but did not say anything.

Mr. Yoshida came into the classroom a little earlier for the second period. He was holding a sheet of paper. I immediately knew it was my test sheet.

As soon as the teacher came into the classroom kids were supposed to stand up and bow to the teacher before every period. All the kids were up and ready but Mr. Yoshida just waved his hands and told us to sit down.

"Nobuo, come over here," Mr. Yoshida called.

I slowly walked up the isle to the front of the room.

"You did not answer any of the questions." He was waving my test sheet. "What do you want to prove by doing this?"

"I don't want to prove anything," I mumbled. I could see he was really angry, veins were showing up on his face. "I just didn't feel like writing the answers."

Our eyes met, and the next moment I almost blacked out. He had slapped my face so hard that I stumbled, but did not fall down.

"This is an insult not only to me but also to the school and the program we've been trying to build for every one of you to learn," Mr. Yoshida was yelling.

The left side of my face was numb but at the same time I was feeling pain; it was a very weird feeling. I was trying to hold back my tears, tears not because of the pain or sadness but because of the boiling hatred for this man which had stirred up in my stomach and had taken over my entire body.

'I won't answer any questions on tests from now on,' I swore to myself. 'I will write a big x on the next one.'

After lunch I did not want to go outside. So I sat at my desk doing nothing but a teacher came around and told me to get out. He stayed until he made sure I was out of the classroom. I went near the sandbox under the cherry trees and sat on the bench. Saburo came and sat next to me. I did not pay attention to him and he did not say a word.

The afternoon classes went uneventfully but very slowly and when it was finally over Saburo asked me if I wanted to go to the river. I said no and headed home.

When I got home I wanted to crawl into the futon closet but mother was there watching so I could not do that. She was getting hysterical because my two brothers were chasing each other around the house screaming. She kept telling them to go outside but they were not listening. I went out and sat on the bench by the side of the house, and looked up. I noticed for the first time that the sky looked different here; it did not have the vastness I had seen by the river and it did not even have the depth.

'What happens if you die?' Out of the blue the thought came to my mind. Some say that the body dies but the spirit remains in the air. Some say you go to another world when you die. Others say that you are finished if you die, no heaven or hell and no spirit in the air flying around either. I wondered what happened to Harumi. I knew that her body was cremated and the ashes were buried under the rocks. 'Is her spirit flying in the air sometimes watching me, or has she gone to heaven where she is having a good time and forgotten about me?

Father came home early. He went into the house and a little later came out and sat on the bench. I did not want to talk to him, so I stood up.

"Listen Nobuo, Mother has found an English teacher for you," father said. "We should go and see him. He lives not too far from here."

I thought it was better than sitting around and doing nothing so I decided to follow him. We walked past the train station, and went over the crossing to the other side of the railroad track. Soon we came to the area where there were several very old houses which had apparently survived the bombing during the war. Father stopped in front of one of the houses and looked at the name plate imbedded on the stone column. It said *Sasaki*.

An old lady came out and greeted us. She led us to a six tatami room overlooking a garden with a man-made pond where several large red and white Koi carp were swimming around. There were stacks of books placed here and there on the tatami floor in the room which did not match very well with the manicured Japanese garden and the Koi-pond. A middle aged man, to me anyone who looked older than twenty five was middle aged, came into the room and greeted my father. The man's name was Mr. Sasaki and he said that he worked for the Yomiuri, one of the three largest national newspapers in Japan. Father introduced me to Mr. Sasaki as his oldest son and told him I was good with art. I did not like that so I made a face. The old lady brought us some tea.

"Mother, bring some beer for us and do we have cold *Ramune* for Nobuo?" *Ramune* was a strongly carbonated drink in a thick glass bottle with a glass ball as a cap. To open the cap, you had to press the glass ball into the bottle. I loved this drink. The lady took back the tray with the tea cups on it and brought a large bottle of beer with two glasses, and a bottle of *Ramune* for me.

"You have quite a collection of gorgeous Koi-carp," looking out at the garden father said.

"Well, it was my late father's hobby. I don't know anything about Koi and how to enjoy them. They cost so much money to maintain and I don't know what to do with them," said Mr. Sasaki as he poured beer into the glasses. "Because my father was so proud of them, I just can't get rid of them, either."

I tried to open the bottle of *Ramune*, but it was so hard that I had to stand on my knees to press it down into the bottle. The bubbles dashed out when I finally succeeded. I had to put my mouth on the bottle to stop the bubbles from spilling onto the table.

As I was drinking *Ramune*, I noticed a thick book which was lying on the tatami near the table which looked like it was written in English. The illustration caught my eye. It was a hardcover and the twisted body of a man and his shadow were drawn in the center of the cover under the title.

"Oh, this is *The Sound and the Fury* by William Faulkner," Mr. Sasaki picked up the book and said. "It's one of the greatest American novels, I believe, but my friend told me that the Japanese translation didn't have the intensity of the original, and he lent this to me. It is not an easy book but someday I hope you will read it in English."

He also said that his newspaper company had been planning to invite Faulkner to Japan and it looked like it would happen in the following year.

"I don't know a word of English and don't know much about American literature, but I did read the Japanese translation of the book," my father said, and they started to talk about literature, American, European and finally Japanese literature which my father loved most and knew best. I never saw my father talking so much, and I was surprised that he knew so much about literature and seemed to enjoy talking about it. He hardly drank alcohol in the house either. So I wondered if he was drunk.

After the lengthy discussion with my father about literature, Mr. Sasaki turned to me and explained about his English teaching. He said that he enjoyed teaching young people, in fact he had five students; three were in high school and two were middle school students, and he had another beginner he wanted to teach together with me.

"The boy has a passion for art like you," he said. "I've seen his oil paintings, he is quite good. He is a freshman at the Ohmori Seventh Middle School. He is a year older than you but you two will be good friends, I can tell."

Mr. Sasaki said that he could not speak English so there would be no conversation, but he would emphasize grammar and along with it, reading and writing.

"In order to master English, I think learning the structure of the language is the most important thing," he said.

We were heading home. It was getting dark and I was hungry. I liked the teacher and it was exciting that at last I would learn English properly which I wanted to do so much, and also I was curious about this boy I was going to study with. 'He is just a year older than me and he paints in oil!' I was impressed and I really wanted to see his work.

"I like Mr. Sasaki," said my father. He seemed to be relaxed and happy. "He must be a good teacher."

We reached our home and when I opened the sliding door, it was dark inside and very quiet as if nobody was home. I thought it was strange; it was way past our normal dinner time and everyone should be home. I opened the fusuma door to the back room.

"Happy birthday!" The light was turned on and mother, Michiko, Hisako, Isao and Tomo were all sitting around the extended dinner table, and shouted. On the table there were tempuras, tuna sashimi and a beef sukiyaki pot which was ready on the electric range. It was an incredible feast in our house. I had no memories of having had such a dinner before. I was stunned and didn't know how to react. I just sat down and could not even smile.

"Look at him!" Michiko yelled. "We worked so hard to make him happy but Nobuo is as grumpy as can be." She stood up and went to the next room, shut the fusuma and started to cry. This was another shocker to me. I really didn't understand what was going on.

"Michiko organized this dinner," mother said to me. "She even bought a cake for you with her own money. She was worried because your spirit has been down lately and she wanted to cheer you up. She told everyone we should not be upset no matter how badly you behaved."

"But Michiko is the only one who got upset," I said and started to eat. I was very hungry and didn't care about Michiko's behavior.

Michiko was always like that, I thought, she was too emotional and too self-absorbed and she was overly sensitive and sentimental. Michiko and I did not get along. I did not think she had any talent in music. She thought I did not have any talent in anything and I was just a fat, arrogant and annoying brat. She was a nice big sister to my brothers though. She looked after them and helped them with their homework every day, and she was even trying to teach them to play piano on the paper keyboard.

Mother went to talk to Michiko and eventually she came back to the table and we all finished eating quietly without any further festivity. It was fine with me.

While we were having tea and eating the cake Michiko brought father a rectangular box which he then handed to me. It was heavy and covered with pretty wrapping paper. I ripped the paper off and I found a wooden

123

case, which I recognized immediately as an oil painting set I had been dreaming of owning. But somehow I did not feel any excitement and did not feel like opening it to see what was inside either. I just kept looking at it for a while.

"Aren't you going to open it?" said my father.

"Thank you," I turned to my father and said. "I will open it later."

Father looked surprised and then disappointed. He tried to say something but swallowed the words.

Many days later, he told me that Harumi's parents had returned the money I had given as a condolence gift and father added some and bought the oil painting set. Also, Harumi's parents brought a folding easel for me, saying that Harumi asked them to get two easels because she and I would need them after the operation to make a big painting together.

A small black swirl was spinning in the corner of the room. It was not growing bigger, but spinning very fast making a humming noise. I kept my eyes on it. Then I noticed there was another one starting a few feet away, the same size and the same speed. Then another one, then another...... Now there were tens of them spinning and flying in all directions, and the noise was becoming a constant roar. They were coming closer and closer to me. I made fists and readied myself. One flew right by my left ear and I tried to punch it but missed. A bunch of them were coming directly at my face. I swung both my arms at them but I caught none, I was only punching the air. I tried to scream, but I had no voice and just air was coming out of my mouth. I couldn't breathe, I was choking... and I woke up. My entire body was drenched in sweat.

FORTUNE TELLER

I was the last one to leave the classroom after lunch. As I was opening the sliding door Saburo came running to me.

"Three kids are coming looking for you." Saburo was out of breath. "One of them is carrying a baseball bat. You should run to the teachers' room."

"Thanks Saburo, but I'm not running," I said. "You should go. I don't want you to get involved."

'If they are coming with a baseball bat I have to have something to protect myself' I thought and looked around. The only useful thing I could see was a chair. The chairs were made of wood and not so heavy. I could easily lift one with two hands and swing it, but how quickly was the question. 'I should definitely attack them before any of them make a move.' That was my conclusion.

I kept the door open and stood about ten feet from it and placed a chair in front of me. Saburo was still hanging around. I gestured to him to get out and he disappeared. Three kids came to the door and peeked inside and saw me, and stepped back probably because they did not expect me to be standing there to greet them. The kid with a bat walked into the room slowly and the other two were right behind him. I waited until all of them were in the room.

"You'll pay for what you did to my brother," the kid with the bat said coming closer to me but the bat was hanging from his right hand and resting on the floor. I was holding the chair with both hands and ready. The kid came close enough and I lifted the chair and smashed it over his head with all my strength. He did not even have a chance to lift his bat. The chair was smashed into pieces, and he collapsed on the floor and blood started to run from his head and shoulders. I was still holding part of the chair in my hands and turned to the other kid. He was just standing there with his mouth open and looked at me with blank eyes. I dropped the wood and picked up the baseball bat lying by the body of the other boy.

"Stop it, you're going to kill them," someone yelled and held me from behind. I lost my hold on the bat. I shrugged the arms off and turned around and punched him in the face. It was Saburo. Meanwhile, two kids who had attacked me ran out into the hallway. I picked up the bat and ran after them but I was tackled from behind and held on the hallway floor by a big man. I struggled to free myself but I could not move, so I gave up. It was the teacher who had chased me out of the classroom the day before. I was not resisting but he held me down for quite some time, and then two other teachers came running with a school nurse. They went into the classroom.

"Call an ambulance! Call an ambulance!" I heard the nurse screaming.

Two male teachers held my arms and I was dragged down the staircase and the hallway to the principal's office. There, they sat me on a chair but were still holding my arms tightly standing on both sides of me.

I felt strong pain in my arms so I shook my shoulders, but then they gripped my arms tighter. There was no sign of the principal. I heard the ambulance's siren becoming louder and louder, and then it stopped. A policeman came into the room and one of the teachers who was holding me asked him to handcuff me to the chair. The policeman looked at me and laughed.

"I can't do that, he is a minor," the policeman said. "He doesn't look like he's going anywhere. Turn him loose."

"Okay, he is all yours," said one of the teachers and both of them took their hands off me. The pain still remained on both my arms.

Mr. Yoshida came into the room and told the other teachers that he would take over. The two teachers left the room. The policeman told Mr. Yoshida that he needed to take a statement from me. Mr. Yoshida suggested that we should go to his classroom where they could have more privacy since the afternoon classes were cancelled for all six graders. He led the policeman and me to our classroom. I was surprised to see that the blood and broken chair were all cleaned up and the room looked just as normal as could be. Mr. Yoshida brought three chairs to the front of the room, and we all sat down. The policeman asked me my name, age and address.

"Tell me what happened," the policeman asked.

"Three kids came looking for me, and one of them had a baseball bat so I defended myself with a chair," I said.

"That's exactly what Saburo told me," Mr. Yoshida said.

"Who's Saburo?" the policeman asked as he was taking notes.

"A kid in the class and he witnessed the incident," Mr. Yoshida answered.

"Can I talk to him if it becomes necessary?" the policeman asked.

"Yes, I'll make arrangements when you need to speak to him," said Mr. Yoshida.

"Why did those three kids come after you?" the policeman asked. I knew the question was coming.

I got up early in the morning for a change. I did not want to be late for school and confront Mr. Yoshida again. I came to the corner where Harumi and I used to meet. I knew very well that Harumi was gone and would never be there to meet me, but still I had to stop and look toward her house. Then those four kids came passing by.

"What are you waiting for?" one of them yelled at me. "She won't be coming."

"You killed your wife, didn't you?" the other one said and they all started to run.

I ran after them in a rage and soon I caught up with the smallest kid. I grabbed his backpack and threw him into the gutter on the side of the street. The kid was dunked in the filthy water and was crying.

Those days in Tokyo where we lived there was no underground sewer system. Human excrement was scooped up from the toilet bottom from outside by a man, who carried it in two pails hanging from a long wood beam tapered on both ends. The man was paid for his service and he sold the excrement to the farmers nearby and the farmers used it as fertilizer to grow vegetables. The water from kitchens and bathrooms was released into the gutters which were mini-canals dug on both sides of the streets.

The other three kids kept running, I ran after them but couldn't catch up. I knew that I was going to have a showdown with them sometime.

"They had been teasing me and my friend, who died a week ago for a long time," I said.

"All right, good enough," the policeman stood up and said to Mr. Yoshida. "We will contact you as soon as the investigation is concluded."

It was quick.

"You punched Saburo, but why?" as soon as the police left the room Mr. Yoshida asked me.

"I didn't know it was him," I said. "Someone grabbed me from behind so I turned around and punched him."

"Do you think Harumi would have approved of your actions?" said Mr. Yoshida looking at me as if he were examining my face.

"That's not fair!" I yelled. His question made me extremely angry.

"Think about it," he demanded and stood up. "Don't move, I'll be back."

Mr. Yoshida left the room and I began to cry. I did not know why but I could not stop. I knew Harumi wouldn't have approved of my actions She probably would have condemned what I had done. But I thought this sort of question was meaningless because Harumi was no longer here. If Harumi were still alive none of this would have happened and I would not have been bothered by those jerks' teasing so much.

"Good news," Mr. Yoshida came back and said. "Hideo is all right, he had a minor concussion but his injuries are minor. He will be released from the hospital soon."

Hideo was the kid with the baseball bat. I didn't care what happened to him but Mr. Yoshida looked relieved and happy.

"Your mother is on her way to pick you up," Mr. Yoshida said matter-of-factly.

"Why? I could go home myself," I screamed. The last person I wanted to see right now was my mother. I was in no way ready to deal with her emotional reaction to this.

"I cannot just let you go home," said Mr. Yoshida. "There will be an emergency faculty meeting later. You guys have done some serious damage here, you know that."

Mother came all dressed up in a kimono. Mr. Yoshida greeted her at the door and they went somewhere leaving me alone in the room. I went by the window and looked down at the school yard. The classes must have been over; kids were going home. All of a sudden I was struck by fatigue. Mentally and physically I was exhausted and wanted to go home. I sat on the floor and leaned against the wall. Mr. Yoshida and mother were taking too long.

"Nobuo, Nobuo, we can go home now." I thought I heard my mother's voice but for a few moments, I was disoriented and didn't know where I was. I must have fallen asleep. Mr. Yoshida helped me to get up.

On the way home mother was very quiet; she did not nag me as I expected. I did not have anything to say to her either, so we were just walking along without a word for a long time. But when I looked up and saw her face I realized that she was in pain. Her teary eyes and the deep wrinkles between her eyebrows were showing her agony. Only then did it strike me. The look on my mother's face reflected the seriousness of what I had done in school. I did not want to see my mother like that. I felt guilty and miserable. I wished she were yelling at me and nagging me all the way home.

"You don't have to go to school for a few days," mother said just before we reached home.

"You mean, I was suspended?" I said and wondered if the other kids were suspended also. "For how long?"

"I don't know, but your father and I must go to school for a meeting on Saturday," mother muttered. "We will have to see the principal and the parents of the other children."

I could not sleep. It was past ten o'clock. Mother opened the fusuma door and saw us all asleep, but I was only pretending. The fusuma was closed and she started to talk to father. I could not hear well but I knew she was talking about me. "...such violence..." I heard her saying. "...no discipline..." I did not hear my father's voice. "It's your fault." I covered my ears with both hands, and closed my eyes.

I saw a big white cloud floating in the sky like a mountain or island moving ever so gently. As I was watching, the top of the cloud gradually glowed in gold and trees, houses and the people were illuminated. I saw a little girl with a bright yellow dress on top of the rock. She was waving her hand to me and calling; "come over here, Nobuo, hurry and come here!" I ran, ran as fast as I could but I wasn't getting any closer to her. Still I ran.... I ran until I was completely exhausted and collapsed. I was wet and smelly. I looked at myself; half my body was in the gutter. I looked up and saw the girl with a yellow dress falling from the rock. I wanted to catch her but she was out of reach. "Nobuooo....," I heard her cry out my name. Suddenly the cloud became black and spinning. It became a humongous swirl and was moving around me. I was readying myself for attack. It came right at me from the front, and I threw my body, tackled it down and held it tight to the ground. To my surprise it did not struggle and then it was becoming mushy. I tried to squeeze it tighter but it became inflated and started to embrace me, and soon my entire body was inside of it, so soft and comfortable. I thought I finally reached the cloud.

When I woke up in the morning, the house was very quiet. I did not want to get up, so I stayed on the futon. I thought it was really great that the school had suspended me; they gave me a vacation which I needed so badly. I was getting bored so I crawled out of the futon. I opened the fusuma to the next room. I expected my mother to be there but she was not, but I saw the breakfast ready on the table. I opened the glass sliding door to the garden. It was drizzling and obviously she was not there either. I did not like the month of June because it rained a lot. Almost every day was gloomy and humid. I wondered if it was raining when I was born. I ate breakfast and lay on the tatami floor. I heard the glass door opening.

"Nobuo, you are up." It was mother. "Good, you finished your breakfast too. I want to take you to a fortune teller."

"What, fortune teller?" I said.

"Yes, put your futon back in the closet." She took the dishes away and was cleaning the table.

I went to the next room. I folded the futon comforter and took it to the closet and then came back and folded the futon mattress and put it in the closet.

"Why are you taking me to a fortune teller?" on the way to the station I asked my mother. The rain was tapering off.

"Because I am worried about your future," she said.

"This fortune teller will make my future better?" I couldn't help being sarcastic.

"No, but we could be prepared if he could tell us what lies ahead," mother said. "For instance, he may tell us how the meeting is going to turn out tomorrow." She was talking about the scheduled meeting with the principal, Mr. Yoshida with a few other teachers, the parents of the other three children and my parents. "They might decide to send you to reform school."

"That's all right, I will go wherever they want me to go," I said. I really did not care. Actually I was curious about reform school.

We had to take two trains and a bus to get to the place. I knew we were out of Tokyo but had no idea where we were. From the bus stop we walked on a dirt road for a few minutes and came to a very old house. Inside the wood framed glass doors there was a room with a dirt floor. There was a large square table in the center of the room and wooden benches were placed against three walls. Several people were waiting on the benches. I did not see any children, but of course it was Friday morning.

We were waiting for quite some time and I became restless and hungry.

"You have no patience," mother mumbled, and took out three Japanese pastries. I gobbled them up and stood up. There were more people coming into the room. Mother held my hand and told me to sit down.

Finally it was our turn. A young woman came and led us through a narrow corridor to a small area with a wooden floor and opened the fusuma door. Mother told me to wait there and went into the room. I had to wait again; I hated waiting as mother said I did not have patience. Several minutes later mother opened the fusuma and told me to come in.

An old man with long white hair and a beard was sitting behind a thick wooden table. He was wearing a white linen kimono, looking like *sennin*, a hermit in the mountain. I felt like I was on a small theater stage.

"Come closer, young man," the old man said. I moved closer to the table on my knees. He gazed at my face for a few minutes with sharp eyes. I stared back at him.

"Um....," he turned to my mother and said, "I like this boy, strong mind, gentle and kind heart." He said it as if he were reciting Chinese poetry. I thought it was funny.

"I don't know about the gentle and kind part, but he is a stubborn child," mother said smiling.

"Show me your hands," the old man asked me. I put both hands on the table. He took my right hand and stared at the palm for a few seconds, and then the left hand. He held both my hands and examined and compared them for a few minutes.

"He must have had a rough time these past few years but he will be fine from next year on," the man was talking to mother, not to me. "He will thrive in the middle school."

"What about tomorrow?" mother asked hesitantly.

"Tomorrow? Oh, the meeting, not a problem; everything will be fine. Someone will defend your son," said the man, and he looked at my palms again.

"I cannot think of anybody who will defend him." Mother was not convinced.

"Only one thing I am concerned about your boy." Without taking his eyes from my palms the old man said, "He might not have a long life."

This reminded me: Many years ago when I was five or six years old, mother took me to another fortune teller. She was an old lady and she said that probably I would not live past forty. She also said that I would leave home at a young age and would not come back. I remember that my mother was very upset and told me she would never go back to her.

"He will experience a life or death situation in his late thirties or early forties," he continued. "But if he survives this crisis, he will have a long life."

Mother looked stunned and was speechless. I thought it was quite an improvement from the old lady's prediction.

"He has potential to be somebody, might accomplish something important but he needs to be free, so don't try to tie him down. A big fish needs a big ocean to live." The man took a deep breath and concluded. "I believe your son will have a rather short but exciting life."

'Short but exciting life.' I loved it.

BIGGEST FOOL ON EARTH

Mother was frantic the next morning. The meeting was scheduled for afternoon but she was getting ready to go right after breakfast. She was looking for a pair of earrings, opening every drawer in the cabinet when they were sitting right on the table where she had put them earlier. She was obviously worried. When I came into the kitchen to get a glass of water I saw her standing by the sink looking at the ceiling with tears in her eyes. I felt guilty for putting her in this situation. But what about the fortune teller? He told mother not to worry, everything would be fine, but apparently she did not believe him at all. Then why did she go to him forcing me to tag along?

Father came home around noon and had lunch with us quietly. He never asked me about what had happened in school. He did not say anything about the meeting and showed no reaction to the matter whatsoever; no anger, no distress and not even a speck of worry. I thought it was the sign of ultimate indifference. It was fine with me, actually I liked it. I did not want both mother and father going crazy over my affair.

They left home around one o'clock. Before leaving, father reminded me of the English lesson. Mr. Sasaki was going to give me and another boy lessons twice a week on Wednesdays and Saturdays. Today was the first day. I was supposed to be at Mr. Sasaki's house at two o'clock.

I arrived a little early and the other boy was not there yet, but Mr. Sasaki was already home. He invited me to sit on the stone bench by the pond.

"How is school? Are you having fun?" he asked me as he was sitting next to me.

"It sucks. I'm not having fun at all," I said. "I don't like school and the school doesn't like me."

"I thought you were a good student. I saw your report card." Mr. Sasaki looked surprised.

"The school work is easy but everything else is so hard," I said. I almost told him that I had been suspended but I swallowed the words. I did not want to explain to him what had happened.

The boy showed up and that saved me from further questioning by Mr. Sasaki. His name was Takeo. He was about my height, slim and sporty looking and seemed to be a nice kid. We were led to a small tatami room with a low rectangular table in the center. Takeo and I sat side by side on the tatami at one side of the table, facing Mr. Sasaki.

Mr. Sasaki wrote simple vowels; *a ,e, i, o, u* and double vowels such as *ei, ai, au, ou...* on the paper and showed us how to pronounce them, Then he wrote down simple words which contained those vowels such as busy, many, mouth, boat, horse....., twenty of them with Japanese translations. He told us to copy those words into our notebooks.

"Try to memorize these words. I will give you thirty minutes," said Mr. Sasaki and left the room.

I knew most of the words and their meanings in Japanese but I had no idea how to memorize spellings. Takeo started to write each word repeatedly, saying each word orally. So I did the same. Mr. Sasaki came back soon enough.

"How are you doing?" he said as he was sitting down. Takeo smiled and nodded.

"I know those words but I have trouble with spelling," I said. "I have no clue how to remember."

"All right, let's see," said Mr. Sasaki and then he gave us blank sheets of paper and started reading the words. I tried to write them down but I knew they were not correct.

It turned out that I spelled two words out of twenty correctly; cat and book, but the meanings in Japanese were all correct. Takeo had three wrong spellings and did not know the meanings of five words. Mr. Sasaki told us to study those words at home, and he would test us on Wednesday again. He told me to write and say each word until my hand remembers the spelling. He also gave me a textbook which was used in the middle school Takeo was attending. He said that Takeo's class had studied about twenty five pages of the book, so he would have to bring me to that point first. This was worse than remembering how to write Kanji. I felt like I was a complete fool and I said that to Takeo as we were leaving. He said that he had trouble at the beginning also and I would be fine.

"You paint in oil," I said to Takeo. We were on the street. "Mr. Sasaki said you were very good."

"Yeah, I do. Do you paint in oil too? Takeo asked.

"No, I have a set but haven't tried yet," I said. "Who is your favorite artist?"

"Matisse!" He exclaimed. "Who's your favorite?"

"Cezanne, I guess, I don't know... I like Klee too," I said. "Can I see your paintings sometime?"

"Sure," he said. "That's my house."

We had only walked two blocks. The house looked big surrounded by tall trees. He said that he wanted to show me his paintings but he had to go somewhere today. He asked me if I could come and visit him tomorrow. I said I would come after lunch.

Mother and father were already back when I arrived home. Mother was smiling and talking with my sisters. I knew the meeting had gone well for me. Father was about to leave the house. He said that he had to go to a meeting of his own at work.

"I learned something today." This was the first thing mother said when she saw me. "A teacher, principal or even the police cannot send a child to reform school. You need a court order to do that."

There was no counselor in the school in those days in Japan and there was no child psychiatrist or psychologist available. Even if such services ever existed, they were not available to ordinary families, so any children with emotional or psychological problems were treated as children with behavioral problems. The family court routinely sent those children to an institution called *Shounen-in*, the direct translation of which is *boy institute*, namely reform school.

"The fortune teller was right, incredible!" mother said. "Mr. Yoshida defended you from the beginning to the end."

Now the fortune teller was mother's hero. She did not want to believe a word he said until this morning.

"Mr. Yoshida said you initiated some kind of program to help other children in the school."

"What?" I could not believe what I heard. "I never started any program in the school, let alone anything to do with other children. Do you think I would do such a thing?" I did not think Mr. Yoshida would make up a story like that to defend me.

"Well, that's what Mr. Yoshida said."

According to my mother the meeting went like this:

Mr. Yoshida summarized the incident, starting from the days when

Hideo, his brother and two other kids kept teasing Harumi and me on the street. Then the principal read the police report which said that they did not find any reason to get involved. There was excessive violence on my part which they were very concerned about, but under the circumstances where three boys came to attack me with a baseball bat in their hands, my action was justified. Hideo's parents insisted that Hideo was carrying a baseball bat but never intended to hit me. Mr. Yoshida raised a question; then why did they go all the way to the equipment room to get the bat and then come back to the classroom looking for me? He also mentioned that there was a witness who heard Hideo saying to the other two boys that he wanted to smash my head with the bat. Hideo's parents wanted the school to send me to Shounenin, but the principal explained that the school did not have such authority, even if they found me to be unfit to be in the school setting. Only the court could send a child to an institution. Mr. Yoshida portrayed me as a good student who was academically at the top of the class and who had even initiated a program to help other children. Hideo's parents looked very surprised to hear this, and finally shut up.

"You could go back to school on Monday," mother said.

I woke up in the morning feeling good. I did not want to admit it but the incident and the prospect of what could have been the outcome of yesterday's meeting must have been putting a heavy weight on me. I was also happy to see my mother back to normal. Characteristically, father did not say a word about the meeting.

After lunch I headed to Takeo's house. I thought about bringing some of my work to show him, but then I realized that I had destroyed every one of my recent drawings when I heard of Harumi's death. I had not done anything since, so I had nothing to show.

Takeo greeted me at the door. He took me down a corridor and there was a wood door at the end. As soon as he opened the door the smell of oil paint flowed out of the room. It was so strong, almost intoxicating.

Inside was a rectangular room with a wood floor. It was not a big room with only one tiny window facing out to the woods. A large easel was standing in the middle of the room. There was a floor to ceiling painting rack on one side and the rest of the walls were covered with artwork. Most of them were either still lifes or figures, and all his works looked very much like Matisse's work. I recognized some reproductions of Matisse paintings among the canvases and drawings. The whole room was a celebration of Matisse but it also showed that Takeo was a serious artist. I was overwhelmed by the energy and passion radiating in Takeo's work. I thought I was an infant compared to him. I was glad that I did not have anything to show him.

"You are so good, like a pro," I said. "How long have you been painting in oil?"

"About two years," he answered.

"Is it hard to paint in oil?" I asked.

"Not really, but it took me quite some time to get used to the paint though. My dad showed me everything; how to mix and thin paint, clean brushes and stuff, but it's so different from watercolor, you know."

"Your father is an artist?" I asked.

"Actually he has been a graphic artist for all his life, he works for Matsuya department store." Matsuya was one of the oldest and largest department stores in Tokyo located on Ginza, the commercial center of the city.

"You are so lucky to have your own studio." I was looking around the room carefully.

"Originally this was some kind of storage room, I hear, and my father turned it into a studio and used to paint in here," Takeo said. "He gave up painting during the war and now he lets me use it."

I found a small canvas on the floor leaning against the wall and I went closer and stared at it. It was a landscape, showing rough brushstrokes with thick paint. It was different from any of the other painting in the room.

"Do you like it?" Takeo picked up the painting and asked. "I did it in Vlaminck's style."

"Yes, very much," I said, but I never heard of Vlaminck. "Did you paint this by the Tama River?"

"No, I did it in here but it is based on the sketches I did by the river."

"I used to go to the river every Sunday to draw," I said. "Landscape was my thing, I can't draw figures."

"Not, anymore?" He put the canvas back on the floor. "What are you working on now?

"I haven't done anything lately," I mumbled.

"Why?" asked Takeo, looking at my face.

"I don't know, I just lost interest," I said and turned around and looked at the window.

"Let's go outside," he said and opened the door.

In the hallway we bumped into a young man with very short hair. He was looking down and did not even look at us.

"That's my brother." As we were walking out the door, Takeo said. "He was accepted to Waseda High but he's taking a semester off right now?"

Waseda High School was a private school directly connected to Waseda University which was one of the best private colleges in Tokyo. Since he had been accepted into the high school, he was guaranteed a place in the college.

"What's wrong, is he sick?" I asked.

"Come, I want to show you something." He ignored my question, and ran into the woods. I followed him on the narrow path between trees, and we came to an opening. There was a fairly large tomb about eight feet square. It was built up three layers with blocks of gray stones, and there was an uncharacteristically small rectangular black marble headstone in the center.

"This is my great grandfather's grave," Takeo said and stepped onto the grave and sat on the top. "Come and sit."

I was hesitant because we were taught by our parents that we must respect our ancestors' graves; stepping and sitting on them was not thinkable.

"It's okay," he said. "Great grandfather wanted us to do this."

I sat on the stone.

"Look at this," He put his hand on the headstone and said.

"Takezo Iwata." I read the name engraved in the stone.

"That's him, but look what it says under his name."

There were small letters engraved under the name: 'biggest fool on earth'

"What's this?" I exclaimed.

"You see, our family used to own this whole area including the mountain behind us for hundreds of years," Takeo started to explain. "After he retired in his late fifties, my great grandfather started to gamble. He became a degenerate gambler and lost most of his fortune. He tried to recoup everything he had lost in one shot and gambled away the whole property except this house and the surrounding land. The next morning he came here and committed hara-kiri. He left a will which said to build a grave for him here and place a small gravestone on it, on which the words had to be engraved under his name; 'biggest fool on earth'. He also instructed his son, he had only one child, to come and pee on his grave on every anniversary of his death."

"What an incredible story," I said.

"Isn't it?" said Takeo. "Do you have any brothers or sisters?"

"Yeah, two older sisters and two younger brothers," I answered. "But why?"

"Wow that must be fun, five kids in a house," he said. "I wish I had some sisters and more brothers."

"I don't know about that. We live in a small house, so there is not a moment of peace in the house," I said. "I was just thinking, it would be nice to live in a big house like yours with just one or two siblings."

"My great grandfather was an only child in his family; my grandfather was an only child and my father is also an only child. I have a brother, three years older than I am, but I feel I have been treated like an extra. My brother is very smart, and has always done well in school. My parents, relatives and everyone compare us. Whatever we do, he does better than I do. I think if I had more siblings things would be different."

Come to think of it, we did not have such rivalry between the five of us. Each of us was doing his or her own thing, even between my two sisters whose interests were the same; music.

"But you are better in art, right?" I had to say something.

"Art doesn't count. They think it's just a hobby," Takeo said. "There is one thing though, I am healthier. My brother has been ill too often"

We heard some people talking in a distance.

"My parents are back," Takeo said. "They are Christians, you know; they go to church every Sunday. They used to take me and my brother, but it's so boring, we stopped going."

We walked back to the house. Takeo's father was standing outside of the entryway. Takeo introduced us.

"So nice to meet you." His father had a very gentle voice. "You like to paint, I hear. Why don't you come and paint with Takeo sometime?"

"Good idea, let's go to the Tama River and do some sketches together," Takeo said excitedly.

I was just smiling, but feeling very awkward. I was not ready to go back to the Tama River; I was in no way ready to do any art work, let alone doing sketches with Takeo by the river.

KAMIKAZE SENSEI

I woke up on time, had breakfast and headed to school although I really did not want to go. I came to the corner and I hesitated a moment but stopped and looked toward Harumi's house anyway. I did not see those four kids. They must have changed the route to go to school.

I arrived before the morning assembly. It seemed like the whole school knew what I did to Hideo; kids were avoiding me in the schoolyard. If I looked at them they quickly turned around. A lot of kids were looking at me from afar, and whispering. I knew they were afraid of me. I was some kind of horrible monster now. I became weary and felt my spirit was falling into abyss.

In the classroom kids were acting the same way; they did not look at me.

They were avoiding eye contact. Saburo too was acting differently; he did not say hello to me or look at me. I wanted to apologize for punching him and I wanted to thank him for trying to stop me from going after the kids with the baseball bat. I wondered what would have happened if he did not stop me. The thought gave me a chill. But I did not have the opportunity to talk to him before the class began.

Mr. Yoshida came into the classroom as usual and started the class right away. We were studying ratios; kind of things like percentage, rate, and averages. He said he wanted to review what we had studied the past week.

"Those who know the answer raise your hand," said Mr. Yoshida and he started to ask questions.

I was watching two round clouds floating in the sky through the window. They were drifting together ever so gently keeping the same distance from each other. I could not help thinking about Harumi. A part of me still could not accept her sudden disappearance, her death. I missed her, missed her dreadfully.

"Nobuo, tell me the answer." I heard my name called which brought me back to reality.

"I am sorry, I don't know," I stood up and said. I had no idea what he was asking.

"Don't know the answer or don't know the question?" asked Mr. Yoshida.

"Both, I guess," I mumbled. There was some laughter among the kids.

"You must pay attention to me," he said in a harsh voice. "Sit down."

I could not figure the man out. Mother said he had defended me vehemently at the meeting, yet now he is embarrassing me in front of the whole class like this. I could still feel the pain he had inflicted on me by slapping my face when I had submitted a blank test paper.

Toward the end of lunch time Mr. Yoshida told Hiroshi and me to practice pitching during the break and reminded us that the baseball tournament would start the following week. I finished eating quickly. I had to go down to the equipment room to fetch a catcher's mitt since

I had not brought my glove, but I remained in my seat waiting for an opportunity to speak to Saburo. Most of the kids were already out of the classroom, but Saburo was still finishing up his lunch.

"I am sorry I punched you, I didn't know it was you," I said to Saburo when he stood up. "Also, I want to thank you....."

"Don't say anything, just get your mitt and play catch!" yelled Saburo and smiled. "Do you remember what you said when you gave me notebooks? 'Take them, and don't say anything!' You were scary, scary but nice."

I remembered it very well, but it seemed like ages ago when it happened. Saburo lifted my spirits a little and I appreciated his friendship.

Hiroshi's pitch had improved considerably; his fast ball gained a lot more velocity and it was hurting my hand through the crummy catcher's mitt. His curve ball was breaking impressively on the right spot also. He pitched seriously until the bell.

"Good going, Hiroshi," Mr. Yoshida called out from the bench.

We did not know he was watching. I took the mitt off; my left hand was red and really hurting from catching.

"Let me see the mitt," Mr. Yoshida came over and said. Apparently he saw me shaking my left hand. He took the mitt and examined it.

I tried to pay attention to Mr. Yoshida during the afternoon classes but it was very difficult. My thoughts were flying everywhere; I thought about running away on the freight train. I would have to find out if the train really slowed down before the bridge and if it were possible for me to hop on it. I should visit the Zen temple and see Tadashi soon, I thought. he He said he would show me how to catch crawfish. I thought of the English lesson. I would need to study very hard to catch up with Takeo and show Mr. Sasaki that I was not stupid. I looked out the window; the two clouds were long gone and there was only blank blue space. My thoughts came back to Harumi. What if I were dead and she were alive, I wondered, would she have been as confused as I have been? Still, she would have handled it much better than I for sure.

The last period was science. We were studying 'life science'. Mr. Yoshida was talking about the smallest animal as *amoeba* and *slipper animalcules*. It did not interest me and soon I was drifting into my own world.

"Do you have any questions? Mr. Yoshida said to the class. "Any questions about *life*?"

Without much thinking I raised my hand. I had a question about *life* I had wanted to ask somebody for some time. Mr. Yoshida pointed at me, and I stood up.

"Why do we have to live if we all end up dead?"

Mr. Yoshida looked taken aback by the question and he was silent for a few moments.

"Well, your question is not related to what we have been studying and I want to think about it before I give you my answer," said Mr. Yoshida. He seemed to be choosing his words carefully. "Stay in the classroom after dismissal. I want to talk to you."

'I shouldn't have asked such a question.' I regretted it. I became wary of talking to him face to face. 'He does not have the answer anyway. What is he going to do; is he going to lecture me?' I wondered.

I remained at my desk after the bell. Mr. Yoshida said he would be back and left the room. Saburo was sitting at the desk also. He put the science textbook in his backpack and he took out something else. I thought he was going to do homework, but I did not know what the homework was, or if there was any. I noticed that several other kids were remaining at their desks. Yousuke was there, of course, but so were Kazuo and even Toshio. Kyoko came in with three other girls.

"What's going on?" I whispered to Saburo.

"This is the homework club you started," said Saburo laughing quietly.

Mr. Yoshida came back and asked me to come with him. As we were leaving more kids were coming into the room. We saw Ms. Takano, the teacher of the next class coming in also.

"Let's go to the river, we could talk quietly," Mr. Yoshida said.

We walked down the staircase and were out of the school building.

"Did you see what has become of what you started?" Mr. Yoshida said as he was putting his arm around my shoulders. "At the emergency faculty meeting after that incident, I brought up what you had been doing with a few other children in the classroom after school; doing homework together and mentoring them. I explained to them that many students didn't have room or time to do homework at home. Other teachers liked your idea, and we decided to make it a school-wide program. We decided to open one classroom for each grade for forty-five minutes after school, and teachers will take turns supervising the group from Monday to Friday every week."

"I don't think I deserve credit for that," I shook his arm off my shoulders and faced Mr. Yoshida and said. "It was Harumi and Saburo who wanted to help other children. I was against it; I wanted to keep it for just the three of us, and also I didn't mentor anybody, Harumi was mentoring everyone."

"But you started the whole thing by helping Saburo; isn't that a fact?"

We were at the slope of the dike. We climbed on the slippery wet grass, and we were on the top. I took a deep breath. With the clear sky and gentle breeze, I instantly felt refreshed. Mr. Yoshida went a few steps down to the river side of the slope, and he asked me to sit down.

"I know you kids are calling me Kamikaze Sensei behind my back," as we were sitting down on the middle of the slope Mr. Yoshida said with a faint smile. "I tell you what, it's true. I was a Kamikaze pilot." He looked toward the river. "Then you must wonder why I am still here."

"There weren't enough airplanes," I said without raising my face. I was looking down at the grass. The grass was wet and moisture was seeping through my pants making me very uncomfortable.

"That's right, eighteen of us fighter pilots were stationed at the southern end of Kyushu Island, and there were only twelve planes. The enemy forces were attacking Okinawa Islands, and we were waiting for the order."

"Why are you telling me this?" As soon as I said it, I regretted my outburst and looked at Mr. Yoshida. I thought I would be slapped. Children were not supposed to question teachers; when teachers spoke, you just had to listen. That's the way it was especially with Mr. Yoshida.

"Listen," Mr. Yoshida said calmly as he looked into my eyes. "Let me finish and you will know why I am telling you the story. You are a smart kid, I know, and you are mature enough to understand. It is important not only for you but also for me to tell you my story, okay?"

I nodded. I was relieved that he didn't hit me but I hated the tone of his voice.

"While we were waiting for the order to come, every day was excruciatingly long," Mr. Yoshida continued. "All of us were pretending normalcy but in fact we were suffocating. Some were overwhelmed by fear and frustration and others were irrationally high and excited. I guess I was one of the latter. I couldn't wait to fly my fighter plane into an enemy ship. I would die for my country, I thought; it was the only way to prove my life was worth something. Finally, the order came. It was a beautiful sunny day with cherry blossoms raining petals all over. We were assembled at the airfield, and the commander ordered us to line up in front of him and told us to step forward if we wanted to volunteer for this special mission. Of course all of us stepped forward with no hesitation. The commander nodded approvingly and took out a bunch of chopsticks from his pants' pocket, and explained that since we didn't have enough airplanes for everyone, we were going to have a lottery. He held out the chopsticks and told us that those who picked the ones with a red mark on the tip were the lucky ones and would get the planes. He walked down to the right end of the line, and the first pilot pulled a chopstick. It had a bright red mark on the bottom. "Thank you sir!" he exclaimed. The next man picked the one with a mark also. "Thank you sir!" he screamed, and then it was my turn. I closed my eyes and prayed for luck. When I opened my eyes, I couldn't believe it. The chopstick I pulled didn't have any mark. "Let me try one more time, sir!" I yelled. The commander didn't even look at me; he went to the next person. I really didn't want to be left out. I knew some of the guys had girlfriends, some had aging parents and most of them had some reason to live. I had nothing; my parents were gone and the only brother I had, died soon after my mother passed away. You see, he had contracted polio when he was very young and was permanently paralyzed from the waist down. He knew he couldn't survive by himself. He was brilliant with a passion for writing. He could have been a great writer. He was only seventeen."

There was a silence. Mr. Yoshida was looking at the sky. I heard a whistle blow in the distance. The long freight train was crossing the bridge over the Tama River. It was longer than the bridge; it was a *Home Run* and I cheered quietly.

"Anyhow," Mr. Yoshida took a deep breath. "We had a fairly decent meal that morning for a change, and we were told that we had half an hour before we had to get ready. A cigarette was given to each one of us. We went outside and smoked. Then two of the guys came out with a glove and a catcher's mitt and started to play catch. After several tosses, the guy with a catcher's mitt squatted into a catcher's position and the other started to pitch hard. We all watched intently, and then one guy went behind the catcher and started to act as an umpire. "Strike!" he called out. "Strike!" All of us cheered. The ball hit the ground and bounced into the catcher's mitt. Still, the umpire swung his fist and yelled, "Strike!" We cheered louder. It seemed as if we had forgotten everything, and this simple and pure excitement would go on forever. But it came suddenly. It was time. The catcher walked directly to me and without a word handed me his mitt and the ball. We nodded to each other, and then he was gone. "Yeah, he was a good friend of mine. We went to the same college, and he wanted to be a professional ball player."

"Do you understand?" All of a sudden Mr. Yoshida turned to me and grabbed my shoulders with both hands. I was frightened. "He didn't want to die, you know. Just think how much he wanted to live. How much he wanted to play baseball. Not only him, all of those young men wanted to live. The fact is, nobody wanted to die. I thought I was looking forward to flying into an enemy ship and dying a glorious death, but did I really want to end my life like that? Life, isn't it more precious than that? Isn't it the most precious thing in the world?"

I looked at his face, and I saw his eyes were full of tears. Kamikaze Sensei is crying! It made me shiver and I started to cry also. Mr. Yoshida took his hands off me and turned around toward the river, but the weight and grip of his hands remained on my shoulders.

"I know Harumi was your good friend, maybe the only real friend you have ever had." Looking far away Mr. Yoshida gently put his left arm around me and said, "It must've been a terrible shock to you. I understand, just like my friend left me on the ground and flew away to his death. You asked me in the classroom today, why we must live if we all end up dead. Well, I tell you what, life is beautiful because it ends someday. Look at this little flower." He pointed his finger to a little yellow flower sticking out from the grass by my foot. "It's beautiful isn't it? But if it stays like this forever, do you think it will be as beautiful?"

"Cezanne's paintings don't die and are still beautiful," looking at the flower I mumbled.

"They don't die because they are not alive." Mr. Yoshida squeezed my arm and looked at me. I didn't look up. "Those beautiful paintings were created by a man, and they remain beautiful even after the artist is gone. Mr. Okamoto thinks you are a genius. He told me so, and he has been worried about you a lot."

"I am not a genius!" I said angrily. Mr. Okamoto was our art teacher. Ever since Harumi died, I had been refusing to do anything in the art class. Somehow, I knew for sure that I was not a genius, and I hated to be called a genius.

"But you are talented, everyone knows, and you can't argue about that." Mr. Yoshida squeezed my arm again. I shook my body in protest and he let go. "Don't waste your talent. Don't waste your life away just because your friend died. Harumi had a short life but a beautiful life. Don't you agree? She enjoyed reading, writing poetry and was very happy watching you paint. I think she had a wonderful full life and you were an important part of her life. You owe it to Harumi to live your life in full and be happy. You should leave a lot of beautiful paintings behind so that many, many people could enjoy looking at them for a long time."

"How did you know Harumi was watching me paint?" I thought it was our little secret. I believed that nobody knew Harumi was coming with me when I was painting on the dike of the river. 'Grownups, they are always spying on us.' I thought.

"Harumi's mother told me. She told me how Harumi was looking forward to following you every Sunday." Harumi must have told her mother everything. I didn't tell my parents or anyone anything about Harumi.

"You owe it to Harumi that you live a meaningful and happy life, just like I owe it to my Kamikaze friends whose lives were cut short, and whose chances were taken away. Actually, it was you who taught me this." He poked my shoulder as if to get my attention. "Watching your behavior lately, I realized I had been acting just like you, just like a twelve-year old. It's been nine years since World War II ended, but I was still bitter and angry that I had missed the opportunity to die, and I was acting like I didn't care about anything. I became a teacher only because it was the only job available for me then. I didn't care about you children. It was rather convenient for me that all of you were afraid of me, easier to control, you know. I have been a bad teacher. I was wrong to kick you guys and slap your faces."

I was really shocked by this admission. Who could have imagined that Kamikaze Sensei would say that he was wrong? He had been the terrorizing enforcer in the school.

"I have a proposition to make." Moving his body to the side and directly facing me, Mr. Yoshida said, "I promise I will not hit or kick any children. From now on I will never use physical force on anyone no matter what. So I want you to promise me the same. Violence will not solve any problems, it only makes things worse, and you know that."

I didn't say anything; I didn't want to. But tears were coming down my cheeks like a waterfall and I could not stop it. I was saying to myself that

I would never promise anything like that because I didn't know if I could keep such a promise.

"What do you say, will you promise me?" Mr. Yoshida was standing up.

I shook my head sideways a few times as I was standing up. Mr. Yoshida was straightening up his pants. He turned his back to me for a second and I noticed his pants had a wet mark as if he peed in his pants. It looked so funny that I couldn't help smiling. But I quickly suppressed it as he turned around.

"You devil, I knew you would promise me!" He was laughing. Mr. Yoshida totally misinterpreted my smile. I thought I should protest, but I hesitated for a second and lost my opportunity.

"Do you still have the catcher's mitt? I asked as we were walking back up the slope of the dike.

"Yes I do." Mr. Yoshida put his hand on my head. "Come to think of it, you are a catcher too."

Mr. Yoshida headed back to the school, and I kept walking on the path on top of the dike. Without knowing I was running, cool air was hitting my face refreshingly and I felt as if some heavy weight had been lifted from my shoulders. I couldn't quite comprehend what Mr. Yoshida was telling me, but the image of two Kamikaze pilots playing catch just before heading to certain death was ingrained in my brain and I could not shake it off.

As soon as I reached home, I looked for the wooden case of the oil painting set which was given to me on my birthday, just six days after Harumi's death, but I had never even opened it. When I found it, along with three stretched canvases and a small folding easel under my desk, my heart started to pound. I slowly opened the case feeling as if I were opening a treasure box. It was the most beautiful thing I had ever seen. One large tube of white paint and ten smaller tubes of color paint were neatly lined up in the case, and I found a wooden palette, five different sizes of brushes, two differently shaped knives and a small bottle of oil. I picked up the palette and put my left thumb through the hole and held it tight, and then I took a brush on my right hand as my whole body shivered.

The Catcher's Mitt

"Come and watch Hiroshi pitch; he's awesome," I said to Saburo as I was standing up with my glove under my left arm and the lunch tray in my hands. Saburo was still eating; he was a slow eater.

"I'll see you guys down there," Saburo replied.

Hiroshi was already waiting for me at the door. We ran down the staircase and ran to the cherry trees. When we started to toss the ball for warm up, I saw Mr. Yoshida walking toward us. He was carrying something in his hand, and as he came closer I recognized it was a catcher's mitt. I stopped throwing the ball and waited for him. Without a word he handed it to me.

"Is this the mitt you told me about yesterday? I said and took my glove off my left hand, put it under my arm and received the mitt.

"Yes, this is the one," said Mr. Yoshida.

The mitt was made of light brown leather but the color was faded, and on the outside of the mitt there were scratch marks all over. I took a deep breath and tried to control my emotions. This was the mitt Mr. Yoshida's friend was wearing when he played catch with another pilot. I felt dizzy. I recalled the image of the two Kamikaze pilots pitching intensely and catching a ball before heading to certain death. The image was still overwhelming.

"Do you want to try it on?" Mr. Yoshida said and took my glove from me.

I slipped my hand into the mitt. It was larger than any glove I had ever touched and a lot heavier than my pigskin glove.

"That looks old, is it yours Mr. Yoshida?" Hiroshi was looking at the mitt and asked. I was not aware when he came, but Saburo was standing next to me also.

"My friend gave it to me many years ago. I never used it though. I played outfield, you know," Mr. Yoshida answered.

"Looks awesome!" Saburo exclaimed.

"Why don't you try it?" Mr. Yoshida said to me.

We started to toss the ball. The mitt was soft enough and I had no problem closing it when the ball hit the mitt, but the ball kept falling off. I could not make a firm grip on the ball. I thought that the mitt was too heavy for me.

"Use both hands," Mr. Yoshida called out as he was sitting down on the bench with Saburo.

I supported the glove with my right hand and caught a ball; it did not fall off. I took a catcher's stance and Hiroshi started to pitch hard. It made a heavy thumping sound every time I caught the ball and gave me a strange sensation.

'What was he feeling when he was catching?' I wondered about the Kamikaze pilot. 'He must have been aware that every pitch could have been his last. Every time he caught the ball, did it remind him that he was alive, or was he scared of the next pitch which could be the last?' I was imagining myself in his position, and the thought made me shiver.

"Strike!" All of a sudden I heard Saburo scream from behind me. I was brought back to reality.

"Strike!"

"Ball," Saburo called the next pitch.

"It was a strike," I turned around and complained.

"Too low, it was a ball," Saburo was adamant. "I know what I am doing; I am the umpire."

The pitches called by Saburo added a lot more fun to what Hiroshi and I were doing. I could understand the excitement it must have created when someone took the umpire's roll and started calling the pitches while two Kamikaze pilots were playing catch. All the pitches were called strike, Mr. Yoshida said. Probably no one wanted to hear even one pitch called a ball, it had to be positive, it had to be perfect.

Suddenly the bell rang and we had to stop.

I walked down to Mr. Yoshida and tried to give the mitt back to him. I wanted to thank him for the incredible experience.

"I thought it might be too big for you, but if you could handle it, it's yours," Mr. Yoshida said as he was standing up.

I could not believe my ears, and I was speechless.

"What's the matter, don't you want it?" He was laughing.

"Yes, of course, but this is your...."

"Nobuo." He did not let me finish my sentence. "It's about time for me to say goodbye to my friend, don't you think so? I must move on and so do you."

As we were heading back to the classroom, Hiroshi and Saburo each took turn and tried the mitt.

"It needs some Vaseline," Hiroshi said and I agreed.

"Nice, you are lucky, Nobuo," said Saburo pounding his knuckles on the mitt. "It's too big for me though."

"You keep this." When he gave the mitt back to me I handed my glove to him. "It's not a very good one, pigskin you know, but you could use it, no?"

Saburo stopped and looked at me with disbelief.

"Of course I could use it, but...."

"Take it, and don't say anything!" I yelled and both of us laughed.

As soon as I arrived home, I put Vaseline all over the mitt and rubbed it with a cotton rag. Isao and Tomo were watching me. The mitt became shiny and moist looking, and the color came alive. I smelled the mitt expecting the scent to have changed, and I was disappointed because it did not have the same distinctive smell of the Vaseline on Hiroshi's new glove.

I wanted to show it to mother but she was not around. Isao told me that she went out to have tea with someone. Isao and Tomo wanted to play with me but I told them I must study English, so they would have to wait.

I had been studying English, not only trying to remember the spellings but also studying the textbook Mr. Sasaki had given me. Whenever I had a chance I asked mother or my older sister, Hisako to read a page and translate the sentences into Japanese, and explain what the page was trying to teach. I never asked Michiko, my oldest sister; she was so gentle and patient when she was looking after Isao and Tomo but she did not have patience with me at all. If I asked her the same question twice, she treated me like I was a fool and gave me a lecture instead of an answer. Mother was almost always busy, so I bothered Hisako more often. Mother was strict about pronunciations; she kept correcting our pronunciations when Hisako or I were reading English aloud, especially the distinction between l and r, which we did not have in Japanese. Hisako gave me her old English-Japanese dictionary and showed me how to use it. It was fascinating to see English words lined up on every page of the book and each word was followed by the definition in Japanese. I was very excited to have the dictionary.

I wrote all twenty words Mr. Sasaki had given us correctly from memory, and reviewed several pages of the English textbook. Although I wanted to open the case of the oil painting set and try some paints with a brush, I realized that my brothers were patiently waiting for me, so I took them to the front garden and played sword fighting. After a while I let them win by falling down on the ground and pretending to be dead.

"We killed him, we killed him!" Isao and Tomo screamed.

I realized that it had been a long time since I played with them. I told them to sit on the bench and wait for me and went into the house and brought back a book. It was a Lafcadio Hearn book of ghost stories. Both of them loved the stories, especially Tomo who would scream and yell when the story was coming to the spooky and scary part.

Mother came home and asked me to come inside. My brothers were asking me to read more stories but I told them that was it for the day.

"Mrs. Fujiwara asked me to come for tea, so I went to her house," mother said as she was sitting down at the table. "What a beautiful place they have."

Mrs. Fujiwara was Harumi's mother. My mother was very careful not to mention Harumi's name to me since she died. I thought it was strange that Harumi's mother wanted to see my mother.

"What did you talk about?' I became curious. "About me?"

"She was very worried about you," mother said. "They are inviting you for dinner tonight; will you go?"

"Why?" I said. I really didn't understand why they wanted to see me, let alone to have dinner with me. "What do they want?"

"Oh, she said they just wanted to see if you were all right."

I thought about it. I was kind of wary of meeting with Harumi's parents, but deep inside of me, there was a strong desire to see Harumi's room again. I had this strange feeling that I had forgotten something there, something I don't know but something important, and I must go back and find it. I told mother that I would go.

"They want you to be there around six o'clock," mother said.

"Has it been all set up?" I was upset. "Without asking me first?"

Mother did not answer.

I rang the bell, and Harumi's mother opened the glass sliding door. The drawing I had made with Harumi was still on the wall in the entryway. The elaborate gold leaf frame was overwhelming and the drawing looked rather thin.

"Thank you for coming, we wanted to see you so much," she said. She seemed to be very excited.

"Ojama-shimasu." I took my shoes off, stepped up on the wood floor, knelt, and bowed to her.

"You are always so polite," she said. "You don't need to be in this house."

"Good to see you, Nobuo." Harumi's father came and shook my hand.

Harumi's mother and I sat on the sofa next to each other, and her father sat across from us on the chair.

"We have been worried about you," Harumi's mother said as she was putting her palm over my hand. "We heard you had some trouble at school, so I asked your mother what happened. I am so glad everything turned out all right."

I did not know what to say, so I just smiled. 'Who told them I was in trouble?' I wondered. 'Not only kids in the school, but the whole world must have been talking about what I did with those kids.'

"Those cowards, three of them with a baseball bat!" Harumi's father said. "I heard they were teasing you and Harumi. I am sure Harumi would have been proud of you for what you did."

"I don't think so," I mumbled. "On the contrary, she would have been very upset for what I did to that kid."

"Why is that?" he asked.

"The kid claims he was carrying a bat to scare me, not to attack me. He may be telling the truth. I think I overreacted. Anyhow, what I did to the kid was brutal; I was so angry and lost control. I once promised Harumi I would try not to fight with anyone. I should be ashamed of myself."

The same young woman with a white apron came and said dinner was ready. We all stood up, and the father came and put his arm around me.

"A fine young man, you are. I'm proud of you, son," he muttered.

We walked past the dining room and went into the kitchen, where dinner was prepared on the round table with a white tablecloth.

"There are just three of us, so I thought we would be more comfortable here," the mother said.

There was a large flat pot on the hot plate in the center of the table. I sat on the chair and saw six large fresh oysters on the dish in front of me. I loved fresh oysters, but we could not have them often because they were expensive and we had inadequate refrigeration. The electric refrigerator was not widely available yet. We had an icebox, but we did not always have ice in it, but here in this kitchen, there was a refrigerator taller than I was.

I squeezed a piece of yuzu, Japanese lemon over the oysters and gobbled them up.

"Your mother told me you liked seafood," said Harumi's mother while she took the cover off the pot.

The smell of the seafood was incredible, and made me hungry and very excited. Chunks of fish, clams, crab legs, squid and some fishcakes with white cabbage, scallions, bamboo shoots and shiitake mushrooms were all in a casserole. The mother brought a bowl of rice for me, and I began an assault upon the pot. I did not pay any attention to Harumi's father or mother.

"Very good, healthy appetite," the father said with a big smile when I finished eating.

I was a little bit embarrassed eating like a pig but I didn't care, I enjoyed it.

"Let's have some ice-cream in the living room," said the mother and she stood up.

The woman with the white apron brought ice cream in three small glass bowls to the table in the living room. I had never had ice-cream before. When I had a spoonful of it in my mouth, I closed my eyes and wondered. 'Is there anything that tastes better than this in the world?'

"So, do you want to be an artist when you grow up?" the father asked.

"I like to draw and paint, but I don't know if I want to be an artist," I answered honestly. "I like to write stories too. Actually, I have no idea what I want to be in the future."

"I wanted to be a concert pianist, but the war interrupted my career," the mother said. The grand piano in the living room; it made sense.

"I am an architect now, but when I was a child I wanted to be an archeologist, you know, going around the globe digging up histories."

"Do you design houses?" I asked the father.

"I love designing small houses, but my firm has been busy with a few large projects for the government lately. It's a nice thing that I could participate in rebuilding our country though," the father said.

"Do you still play piano, Mrs. Fujiwara?" I asked.

"Yes, sometimes just for fun," she replied.

"Could you please play *For Elise* for me?"

"Oh, yes." She stood up. "That's right, Harumi played it when you first came here, I remember."

It was not too long ago Harumi played the same tune on the same piano and I was listening, sitting on the same spot on the sofa. My mind went blank listening to the mother playing. The same music beautifully played, same piano and same setting, but it did not bring up any emotion in me, didn't make me sentimental.

The father and I applauded when she was done.

"Can I see Harumi's room?" I stood up and asked when the mother came back to the sofa.

The mother took me to the room. It looked exactly the way it had looked when I came here last time. The only difference was the small drawing in a simple wooden frame sitting on the pillow leaning against the headboard. It was the drawing I made for Harumi to take to the hospital for good luck; the freight train on top of the rainbow and four-leaf clovers on the foreground. It didn't work, did not bring her any luck. The mother noticed that I was staring at the drawing.

"It was the only thing Harumi wanted to take to the hospital," said the mother, and she started to sob. "She asked the nurse to hang it in the recovery room, so that she could see it when she woke up"

"Can I be alone for a few minutes?" I asked. She went out of the room without answering me, and shut the door.

The strange feeling struck me again that I had forgotten something in this room. I looked around the room and wondered. 'Why did I want to see this room? What am I looking for?' I remembered that Harumi and I looked at Klee's paintings on the bed together. Now the book was in my house; she asked me to keep A Picture-Book without Pictures also, and her poetry book. I had not opened any of them since she handed them to me the night before she went to the hospital. Too many things had happened and I completely forgot about those books. Harumi asked me to keep them until she came home, but she did not come home. 'Now what am I supposed to do with them?' I wondered. I opened the fusuma door and turned the light on. The small low table was in the center of the tatami room, and the two square sitting futons were there, just as they were when we sat on them and did the drawing together. Nothing had been moved, nothing had been changed. 'Are they trying to freeze time, and preserve this setting forever?' I wondered. 'But for what? Do they think Harumi's spirit will remain in the room if they keep it this way, or do they need a constant reminder that Harumi once lived here?' I wanted to see the garden, but the shutters were closed and I could not see. I turned the light off and closed the fusuma and sat on the edge of the bed. I was facing the bookshelves. My eyes were gazing at the books without focusing, and I was not thinking about anything, but suddenly I became uneasy and wanted to get out of the room.

"Thank you very much, I had a wonderful time," I said to Mr. and Mrs. Fujiwara as I was leaving.

"We had a very good time too. Please come back soon," said Mrs. Fujiwara and held me in her arms so tight for a long time. It reminded me of the time when she found me on the dike of the Tama River; she held me tight and cried, dropping tears on my cheek. Mr. Fujiwara gave me a strong hug also.

CRAWFISH

After the English lesson, I stopped by Takeo's house. He wanted to show me the painting he had been working on. It was Saturday afternoon and I had no reason to go home in a hurry, and besides, I wanted to see how he cleaned oil paint off the brushes.

A large rectangular canvas was set vertically on the easel in the middle of the room, and in the corner a colorful flower patterned fabric was draped over the round table on which a large tulip shaped white glass vase and a stuffed teddy bear were placed. I thought it was a kind of strange set up. On the canvas, this set up was exaggerated and looked even stranger; the white vase was occupying almost the entire height of the canvas, and the teddy bear was smaller than it actually was so it was out of proportion, but the most striking aspect of the painting was the fabric background; using oil paint directly from the tubes, the flower pattern was painted with thick brush strokes, creating strong contrast to the exploding white vase. I could still see Matisse's influence, but I thought it was an original and powerful painting.

"Fantastic!" I exclaimed. "I like it, great work!"

"Do you think so?" Takeo looked excited. "I like it myself."

Takeo told me that he was thinking of sending it to one of those salons in the fall. There were many French style salons those days in Tokyo; the artists with similar interest in style formed a group and they rented the space in the Tokyo Metropolitan Fine Arts Museum and exhibited their works in the fall and spring. Besides the members' works, they usually exhibited works of nonmembers who wanted to join the group and who submitted their works for the competition.

I had tried to paint with oil a few times in the last several days, but as Takeo warned me, I was having trouble handling the paint; mixing on the pallet, I could not get the right colors, and it was difficult to spread the paint as I wanted. I was very frustrated, but now Takeo gave me an idea that I could apply paint directly from the tubes onto the canvas, and mix the colors on the canvas rather than on the pallet.

I asked him how he cleaned the brushes, and he showed me a metal pot with a cap which was filled with turpentine. He said that the cap had a rubber ring imbedded to seal the pot when it was closed, and there was a metal screen built inside so that the paint dropped to the bottom through the holes and the turpentine was always supposed to be clean. He told me that I could find the pot in the art supply store.

Takeo and his new painting gave me inspiration and encouragement. I wanted to try this technique; applying oil paint directly from the tubes onto the canvas, as soon as I got home.

When I came home, my mother and sisters were sitting around the table and having tea. I put the English textbook and notebook on my desk, and took out the oil paint case, easel and a small canvas from under the desk.

"Nobuo, come and have tea," mother called as I was going out to the garden.

"I am busy," I said standing in the entryway.

"I must talk to you," she said. "It is important."

I put everything down at the door and went into the room.

"Please sit down," she said as she was pouring tea in a cup.

I sat down, but mother was hesitating. I picked up the tea cup and had a sip.

"You like Mr. and Mrs. Fujiwara, don't you?" she asked.

"I do, they are nice people, but why?"

"You are lucky, Nobuo," Hisako said and mother gestured her to be quiet.

"Mrs. Fujiwara came to see me today," mother said. "She said they liked you very much, and....." Mother hesitated again, and I was losing my patience.

"And what?" I said.

"She expressed their strong desire to adopt you," said mother, looking at my face intently as if she was trying to read my expression.

"What, they want to adopt me?" I said. "You've got to be kidding."

"No, she was serious. They love you very much."

This was way beyond my comprehension. They just lost their only daughter, they were keeping her room like a shrine, and now they wanted to adopt and bring me into their lives. "They don't even know me; are they out of their minds?"

"I told her the same; they did not know you. I told her you had an abrasive character; you're short tempered, stubborn, arrogant, disrespectful to adults especially to your parents, have no manners, no discipline and all that, but she just laughed and said they loved you because of all that," mother was smiling. "She said they would do anything to make sure you would have a good and happy life. Oh, they want to build an art studio for you."

"You are so lucky," Hisako said again. "I wish it were me."

"I agree, you are lucky," Michiko joined.

"So, you all want to get rid of me, huh?" I was infuriated. "You want to give me away like old furniture or something."

Tremendous anger and deep sadness had taken over my entire body. Tears were dropping from my eyes. I wanted to scream but my throat was too dry and my voice was not coming out.

"No, not at all Nobuo." Mother looked startled by my reaction. "It's just.... I thought it would be better for you. You could have a much better future..."

I stood up and ran out of the room, kicked the oil paint case and slipped my feet into my sneakers and ran. I came to the corner and stopped. I made a turn and walked toward Fujiwara's house. 'How do they expect me to live in this house with memories of Harumi?' I said to myself as I was passing by the house. 'Do they think I could be Harumi's replacement?'

I came to the dike of the river. Whenever something happened, I always wound up here; the Tama River was my sanctuary. I climbed the stone steps and when I reached the top I took a deep breath. I went several steps down on the slope toward the river and sat down on the grass.

I did not want to live in a big house and I did not need my own studio. Our small house was just fine with me. I did not want to live like a rich kid. I wanted to be with my family, especially with my mother; I could not imagine myself living apart from her. It hurt me so much that she was willing to give me up.

I heard a whistle blow in the distance. The freight train was crossing the bridge over the river. It was a short one, not a *Home Run*, not even close. Not so long ago I tried to run away from here, I wanted to take a free ride on the freight train and go away. I didn't care where to, I just wanted to run away from here, but what was I thinking? I could not have survived if I had done that.

I lay down and looked at the sky. There was no cloud but the sun was setting and I felt as if the vast grey space was swallowing the whole world. I closed my eyes and I became sleepy, but I did not want to make my mother worry, I did not want to have people come looking for me, so I got up and decided to go home.

When I got home, dinner was ready and everyone was sitting at the table. I did not know who put them back, but the easel and other stuff were back under the desk. I sat down quietly and started to eat. Isao and Tomo were fighting over a piece of fish, but no one else was saying anything, and I didn't even look at mother.

After we had finished eating and were having tea, father handed me a cardboard box and asked me to open it. A shiny metal canister was inside; it was a sealable pot for washing brushes. He also gave me a can of turpentine. The only oil which was in the oil paint case was a small bottle of linseed oil. Father saw me trying to wash brushes with it a few days ago, and told me that the oil was not for washing brushes.

The next morning I woke up early while everyone was still sleeping. I did not wash my face or brush my teeth. I tried to take the easel and the paint case out from under my desk which was in the two tatami room behind the entryway. In order to get to it, I had to jump over Michiko's head. I made it, but my left foot touched her temple slightly.

"Ouch!" Michiko screamed. "Nobuo kicked my face!"

"I didn't kick your face, my foot hardly touched you," I yelled.

The commotion woke everyone up. Mother came over and asked what was up but I ignored her and went outside. I set up the easel near the concentration of tall irises which were in full bloom. I went back inside and brought the canvas I had been working on, and the sealable pot and a can of turpentine. I scraped paint off carefully from the canvas with the pallet knife, and took out a tube of purple paint and a round brush from the wooden case. I was thrilled, and painted one petal of the flower with one brush stroke tremulously. After several flowers were painted in the same manner, I washed the brush and took out a tube of yellow paint, and applied it on the center of the petals. After adding a touch of white paint on the yellow and purple, I thought the flowers were coming alive.

"Breakfast is getting cold," Tomo came out for the second time and told me. I was getting hungry too.

I had two bowls of rice, miso soup and some fermented soybean called *natto* with a few pieces of roasted seaweed. As I was finishing up, father came and brought a book of Van Gogh's paintings and opened the page. There was a full page reproduction of the irises painting; a bunch of bluish violet irises were painted on the right half of the canvas, some straight, some twisted and extending toward the center, with the reddish earth. Each delicate flower, each strong and piercing leaf was captured in a living freeze. I gazed at it and studied the picture for quite some time.

I went back to my painting. I painted the leaves in green, yellow and blue, and the ground with yellow, brown and red. I thought it was done and looked good. I sat on the bench and stared at it. After a while, the painting seemed crude and amateurish without any elegance. I stood up and picked up the pallet knife and approached the canvas.

"Don't do that, Nobuo!" the sliding window opened behind me and father called out. I was frightened. "Don't destroy it, you are doing well."

Apparently father had been watching me paint all along through the glass. I turned and looked at father's face, and thought for a few moments. I turned around and with a long stroke I scraped the paint off the center of the canvas. There was a silence and I heard the window close behind me.

After lunch I did not feel like painting anymore, so I was putting the stuff away. Father came and helped me with folding the easel.

"If you have no plan for the afternoon, why don't you visit Tadashi at the temple?" he suggested.

I thought it was a good idea. Father drew a simple map for me to make sure I would not get lost, and gave me money for the train.

Monk Shouzen greeted me at the door.

"Welcome Nobuo, good to see you," he said with a smile, and then he became serious. "I assume you came for meditation, please come in."

"Well...., I came to see Tadashi," I mumbled. "He said he would show me how to catch crawfish."

"Ha ha ha......" he started to laugh. "I know, I know...., I was just joking. Tadashi is not here right now, but he should be back soon."

He took me to the room which was open to the Japanese garden. I remembered that we ate noodles in this room last time. He asked me to sit on the tatami floor at the black lacquered table, and poured tea in a small cup for me.

"How is school?" he asked.

This was usually the first question all the grownups asked me when we met. I hated the question. I always wondered why they could not come up with better questions like 'What are you up to lately?' 'What book are you reading?' or anything but 'How is school?'

"School is pretty bad, I hate it," I spat the words out to him.

"Ha ha ha......" he laughed again. "You hate school; well then, what do you like?"

"I don't like anything." I was ready to go home.

"Ha ha ha..." he laughed again. "I must have offended you somehow. Just like your father when he was young, short tempered and never shy of expressing his feelings."

'My father, short tempered?' I said to myself. I never, ever saw him lose his temper. 'You've got to be kidding.'

"You will like catching crawfish, I tell you." He stood up. "Wait here."

Monk Shouzen came back with a whole dried squid in a little basket, about a four foot long bamboo stick, and some twine. He sat down and ripped the squid into pieces in a basket, and put one in his mouth.

"Um......, this is good, have some?" He put the basket in front of me.

The squid must have been just roasted; it was still hot and smelled delicious. I chewed a piece and savored the flavor.

We walked down to the pond, and Monk Shouzen sat on the rock and tied one end of twine to the bamboo stick and the other end to a piece of squid. The twine was no more than six feet long.

"Throw the squid in the water and wait," he said and handed me the bamboo stick.

I held the end of the stick and cast the twine. It flew slowly into the air and the squid fell into the water with a wimpy splash. It did not even take a minute until I felt a strong tug and the twine was pulled around in the water. I jerked the stick and pulled the twine fast, then I lost it; there was no more resistance.

"Ha ha ha ha....," Monk Shouzen was laughing again. "This is not like usual fishing, there is no hook and so if you feel a tug, you must hold the twine in your hands and pull gently, okay?"

As soon as the squid hit the water, I felt the tug. This time I let it go for a few seconds and grabbed the twine and pulled it slowly. I pulled the crawfish out of the water and it was on the grass, but two huge claws were still holding the squid. I tried to hold it on its back, but instantly it curled up its tail, lifted its claws and attacked my hand. I dropped it on the grass. The crawfish looked angry; its eyes were sticking out and its claws were wide open and ready to snatch anything coming near. It was scary and I was afraid to touch it.

"You hold it here and the claws won't reach you." Monk Shouzen came over and held the crawfish by the end of the body near its tail with his thumb and middle fingers.

He then stroked its head with his forefinger ever so gently. After several strokes, the crawfish lowered its claws and became motionless.

"Now he is asleep," he said and put the crawfish on the grass. "When he

172

wakes up, he will go back to the water.

I caught another one and held it with two fingers. I rubbed its head gently with my forefinger but it did not go to sleep; the crawfish acted more upset than ever. Monk Shouzen took over and promptly made it fall asleep. I tried with every crawfish I caught, but I was never able to put any of them to sleep.

"What am I doing wrong?" I asked Monk Shouzen, getting frustrated.

"Patience, my boy. You must have a meditative mind to make them relaxed."

I gave up and stopped fishing.

One by one, the crawfish woke up and went back to the water. The whole process was fascinating.

I sat next to Monk Shouzen on the rock and ate the rest of the squid.

"How did you meet my father?" I asked. The comment Monk Shouzen made earlier about my father being hot tempered was puzzling me.

"Well, we met in here in the temple," he said. "Many years ago, when we were in our mid-twenties, we were a group of aspiring writers who gathered here once a month. We read what we wrote to each other, and discussed literature, and we published our own little magazines four times a year. One of the original members, a young lady brought your father here one day, and instantly he was one of us. He was articulate, well read and very passionate. He became the spark of the group."

"Are you sure you are talking about my father?" I had to ask. "He never shows passion for anything, I can't believe he ever had passion. He hardly speaks in the house either."

"Oh, yes, it is your father I'm talking about; passionate and excitable," Monk Shouzen continued. "He was writing stories about the under-privileged, the people who were discriminated against or who were struggling to survive."

"What happened then?"

"The lady who brought your father to us got married to some guy, I think, a diplomat or someone working in the government, and about six months later he stopped coming to the meetings. He said he was taking night courses and studying photography, so he did not have time. But before he disappeared, he wrote an autobiographical novel. Everyone liked it and we published it in our magazine. Did you know your father ran away from home when he was nineteen years old?"

"No, I didn't know that. He never told me about himself, nothing." I was really surprised by this; it was unbelievable that he had done such a thing.

"Your father was the oldest son in a very old family who owned a large farm in Aichi Prefecture. He was very smart and did extremely well in elementary school and wanted to go to high school and college, but your grandfather thought a farmer did not need an education. Your father's teacher went to talk to your grandfather and tried to persuade him to send your father to high school, but he refused to listen. He stayed at home for a few years, but could not give up his dream of becoming a writer, so one day he left home and came to Tokyo without telling his father or anyone. His father never forgave him for that."

"Do you still have the magazine?" I became very anxious to read the whole story.

"I think I have it somewhere," Monk Shouzen said. "I will look for it sometime."

"How did you meet him again?" I asked.

"After the war ended and when your family came back to Tokyo, he came to see me. He was already a different person then; calm and very controlled. He was married and had five children. You were about five years old, I believe."

I vaguely remembered that my family escaped Tokyo during the war, and lived in my grandfather's house for a few years, and mother was always very unhappy and hysterical. I had one vivid memory; mother was upset over something I did, and pushed me down the staircase and I landed on a lower level with excruciating pain. According to mother, living with our grandfather was the worst hell for all of us.

"Hey Nobuo, I didn't know you were here." It was Tadashi holding a guitar and walking toward us. "My friend got a new Hank Williams record and I had to go and listen."

"I guess I should leave you guys alone," said Monk Shouzen and he walked away.

We went to Tadashi's hideout.

"You want to hear what I learned today?" Tadashi said and started to play his guitar and sung.

> I was ridin' number nine
> Headin' south from Caroline
> I heard that lone-woh woh- some whistle blow
> Got in trouble had to roam
> Left my gal and left my home
> I heard that lone-woh woh-some whistle blow

"I like that!" I exclaimed and clapped my hands. "The whistle sound you made was incredibly beautiful."

"Thank you, thank you." Tadashi bowed like a musician on the stage. "That sound has to go out through the nose, you know. It's not easy to do."

Ever since my mother told me that Mr. and Mrs. Fujiwara wanted to adopt me, somehow I wanted to see Tadashi and talk about it, but I decided not to bring it up. I did not want to spoil the fun we were having.

When I came home, my brothers were playing sword fighting in the garden, and father was sitting on the bench and reading a book.

"How was it; did you have fun?" father asked.

"Yes, I enjoyed the visit very much," I answered.

'How little I knew my father!' I was thinking as I looked at his face. It was astonishing that I knew nothing about this man, my own father, and I wondered. 'Would I ever be able to really know him?'

"Come and sit, I have something to tell you." Father moved to one side of the bench and made room for me.

"I went to see Fujiwara-san this afternoon and told them the adoption was not possible. They said they did not think it was going to happen, but they loved you like their own child so they had to give it a shot." He looked at me with a smile and continued. "Your mother loves you very much. You must understand. She was thinking about nothing but your future when she considered Fujiwara-san's offer. Your mother grew up in a wealthy family. Her father was the acting president of Meiji University and his family was one of the biggest silk kimono merchants in Kyoto. She knows the difference wealth can make; she thought you could have many more opportunities and a brighter future with them."

GOODBYE

The baseball and volleyball tournaments started on Monday, June 14. For sixth graders, afternoon classes were cancelled on Tuesday and Friday for two weeks and we boys played baseball while the girls played volleyball.

We played the first game against the Class One team. Hiroshi pitched brilliantly and allowed only two hits and no runs in five innings, and our batting exploded; we scored four in the first inning, two in the second inning and four in the fifth inning, and the game was over. There was a mercy rule which called for the game to end if the winning team is ahead by ten runs after four innings. I contributed by hitting a two base hit which made two runners score in the first inning and a home run with two runners on base resulting in three runs in the fifth inning. It was a very exciting game for our team; everyone had a great time.

The second game was against Class Four, the team we had played a practice game against in early May and lost to after Hiroshi's throwing error. It was not as easy as the first game, but we won the game by the score of five to three. Somehow in this game I could not hit; I struck out three times and grounded out twice.

Meanwhile, our girls' volleyball team won the first game and was waiting for the final championship game. There were five classes, five teams, so there were only four games to play in total.

Hiroshi and I watched the game between Class Two and Class Five teams on the following Tuesday. We were going to meet the winner of the game for the championship match. The pitcher of neither team was very sharp, and it became a high scoring game. After the bottom of the seventh inning, the score was eight to six and the Class Two team was winning. At the top of the ninth they added another run and the game ended nine to six. I noticed that there were a couple of good batters on the Class Two team and I mentioned them to Hiroshi. He said he knew but he could handle them.

Hiroshi practiced pitching with me at lunch break and after school for two days, and I thought he was in top shape and ready. He was acting a little nervous before the game, but I thought I could not blame him because after all, it was the championship game.

At the top of the first inning, I was at bat with a runner on second base and with two outs. After hitting a couple of foul balls, I hit a high fly ball to the right field and it looked like it would drop, but the right fielder made an impressive diving catch, and the inning was over.

Hiroshi was impressive from the start; he struck out two batters in seven pitches and he had one ball and two strikes on the third batter. He went for another strike out and threw a fast ball with good speed right over the middle of the plate. The batter swung the bat and the ball flew way over the center fielder. It was a home run. Hiroshi was visibly shaken by this, and he walked the next two batters in a row. Mr. Yoshida asked for time out and tried to calm him down. I reminded Hiroshi that it was just one run, and the game had just started. He seemed to be calmed down, but the next batter had a base hit and two more runs were scored. He took out the next batter with a ground ball to the shortstop and finally the inning was over.

Hiroshi looked crushed and stayed away from us teammates while we were hitting. I wondered if he would ever recover, but the next inning he went out to the mound and pitched fairly well and did not allow any runs. As innings progressed, Hiroshi seemed to have regained his confidence and was pitching stronger, but the problem was our batting. We had some base hits sporadically, but we could not connect them to produce runs.

In the eighth inning, Hiroshi was in trouble again. After one out he walked a batter, hit a batter and allowed a base hit, and a run was scored. It became painful for me to watch him struggling on the pitcher's mound, but we did not have a second pitcher. We had no one to relieve him. To my surprise, he went on to strike out two batters and the inning was over. Some spectators applauded wildly. We managed to score one run in the ninth and we lost the game with the score of four to one. When the game was over, Mr. Yoshida gathered us and congratulated us for completing the game in such a strong fashion.

The good news was that our girls' team won the championship.

After the third try, finally I felt good about the way the iris painting was coming out. The coloration and brush work looked like the Van Gogh's painting but I was excited about the overall looks of it. I visited Takeo and showed it to him. He said that it was a good painting and he liked it, although he noticed Van Gogh's influence right away. He was surprised that I had learned to use oil paint so quickly. I told him that I struggled a lot. I did not see the large canvas he was working on last time I was here, so I asked him about it.

"I was having some problems with it, so I put it away for now," he said.

"I thought it was going great. What happened?" I was quite surprised.

"I'll show you," said Takeo, and he pulled the canvas from the painting rack and brought it over and placed it on the easel.

The painting was a mess; the teddy bear was scraped off, the white glass vase was reworked on a smaller scale, and part of the beautifully rendered flower patterned fabric was scraped off also.

"What did you do, Takeo?" I screamed. I could not help it. "It had been a beautiful, powerful painting."

"I thought so too, but when I finished it, I felt something was not right and it bothered me." He looked at the canvas and scratched his head and continued. "The fabric was too strong and becoming foreground rather than background, and it was fighting with the vase, and the wimpy little teddy bear looked silly, so I scraped that off and thought I should make it bigger....., one thing led to another and before I knew it, there was an uncontrollable mess. I didn't know what to do and couldn't look at it anymore, so I put it away."

We went outside and walked down to the Biggest-Fool-on-Earth's grave, and sat on the stone step.

"I think you are more talented than I," Takeo muttered looking down on the ground. "I could tell from the painting you showed me."

"What are you talking about?" I was really shocked by his remark. "Come on! I am not even close to your level. You are an artist; my hero. I am a beginner, a student."

"Not really, you have something I don't have."

"Do you feel that way because you made a mess out of your good painting?" I asked.

"No, not that. I have this self-doubt; I want to be an artist but I am not sure if I have what it takes to be an artist."

"At least you know what you want to be," I said. "I don't even know if I want to be an artist. I paint just because I want to paint. I don't care if I have a talent or not. I do it as long as I have a desire to do it."

"Maybe that is the right attitude," said Takeo and smiled at me, and changed the subject. "What are you going to do this summer?"

"I have no plan. I will hang around by the Tama River a lot, I guess," I answered. "What about you?"

"I have no plan either. Do you want to meet up by the river, and do some paintings together sometime?"

"Sure, let's do that," I said.

I wanted to go to the bathroom and told Takeo.

"We should do it here," said Takeo and stood up.

We went behind the grave and stood side by side and relieved ourselves aiming at the back of the tomb, and laughed out loud.

Since the excitement of the baseball and volleyball tournaments was gone the school fell back into being the boring, pathetic place it had always been. It was the middle of July, a few weeks from summer vacation. Since that incident when I smashed a kid's head with a chair, nobody dared to tease me or call me *Balloon*. Even classmates did not talk to me unless they had to, except Saburo but Saburo was leaving at the end of the term.

I had resumed my old activity during the classes; holding a book on my lap under the desk and reading. I was reading a collection of Sherlock Holmes stories. I had never read detective stories before. It was a totally new reading experience for me, and I was drawn to it.

Mr. Yoshida did not bother me. I did my homework and my test results were good. It was strange that he had really become a different person since he had promised me on the dike of the river that he would never be violent. He was such a sweet and gentle teacher now. He did not hit children anymore. He never raised his voice. Many of the students were wondering what had happened to him.

One afternoon after classes were over, Mr. Yoshida told us to remain at our seats, and he made an announcement.

"I don't know where to start," he mumbled and looked at the ceiling. "I've always wanted to work with handicapped children, since my younger brother died a tragic death. He had polio when he was little and was paralyzed from the waist down and I watched him suffer." There was a pause, and he canvassed the entire classroom. I avoided eye contact with him. "A new school for handicapped children will be opening in Kawasaki city, across the river and I was offered a job there as a physical education teacher. I wanted to stay here at least until all of you are graduated in March, but then I would lose this opportunity. Well, it wasn't an easy decision but I have decided to take this job."

There was total silence in the classroom, no one said a word.

I was devastated. I had just become close to this man, I thought. Finally there was a grownup that understood me and cared about me. Harumi came into my life from nowhere and quickly became my best friend, and suddenly left me. Saburo is leaving for a new life in Osaka and now Mr. Yoshida is leaving. 'What is this?' I wanted to scream. 'Everyone who has become close to me has either left or was leaving me, how can I take this, how can I go on?'

"I promise you one thing; I will come back to see you on graduation day," he concluded, and we were dismissed.

Mr. Yoshida was standing by the door and talking to some kids. As I was approaching the door, he gestured me to stay, but I ignored him and went by him quickly.

'Why didn't he warn me before making an announcement to the whole class?' I felt betrayed, but then he hadn't warned me when Harumi died either. I was just one of the students to whom he had to break the news.

When I came home, my mother was playing *Koto*.

Koto is a traditional Japanese stringed instrument. It is about seventy one inches in width, and is made of *Kiri*, Japanese cedar wood. There are thirteen strings over thirteen movable bridges along the width of the instrument. Players face the *Koto*, which is placed on the floor and adjust the string pitches by moving these bridges, and use three finger picks on thumb, index finger and middle finger to pluck strings.

Isao and Tomo were sitting in front of her listening. I took my backpack off my shoulder and put it on the tatami floor carefully, and went and sat between my brothers and put my arms around their shoulders. It had been a long time since I heard mother play *Koto*.

"More, more, more...." when she finished, my brothers and I clapped our hands and chanted.

"Nobuo, this is your favorite," said mother and started to play the tune called *Rokudan*, which means sixth level.

The familiar melody had the clear distinctive sound of *Koto*, but somehow it made me melancholy today. I felt a heavy weight in my heart, and it was taking my whole body down.

"Mr. Yoshida is leaving school at the end of the term," I said to mother when she finished playing *Rokudan*.

"Oh my..., really?" She looked very surprised. "He is such a good teacher, he's been so good to you."

I wanted mother to hold me. As I was helping her put away the *Koto*, I had such a strong need for her sympathy, and it made me feel like crying.

"Why don't you give the irises painting to Mr. Yoshida as a farewell gift?" mother suggested.

I thought about it. When he gave me the catcher's mitt Mr. Yoshida said. 'It's about time for me to say *goodbye* to my friend. I must move on and so do you.' At the time he must have known he was leaving. That was why he gave me the mitt. I wanted to give him something back. It was a good idea to give him my painting, but not the irises; it had to be the Tama River. I had two weeks to do the painting.

The following Sunday morning, I woke up early, skipped breakfast and went to the river with a sketchbook and pencils. I wanted to work directly on the canvas with oil paint, but I realized that I could not carry all the necessary stuff to the river by myself, so I decided to do several sketches at the site and work on the canvas from those sketches at home. I drew a few different scenes, but I felt most comfortable with the scene with the bridge and freight train. I concentrated on that scene and tried it from a few different angles, and did some detail sketches of the train and the bridge.

It was already eleven o'clock when I got back home. Breakfast had been cleared from the table. Mother made some udon noodle soup for my brunch. I set up the easel in the front garden and placed a new canvas on it, put the paint case and the sketches on the bench, and I started to work.

Using a charcoal stick, I drew the scenery on the canvas. I did not want to paint an ordinary quiet comfortable landscape. I wanted to make the energy and passion visible on the surface. I started to paint from the foreground; the green field and the dike. It was going very well and I was excited, especially the dirt road on top of the dike, which was winding and stretching to the bridge. It came out beautifully.

I worked until around five o'clock without any break and the painting looked finished. Father came out and commented on it and congratulated me. But somehow I was not very happy about it. I felt something was missing.

I went inside and had some Japanese sweets with a cup of green tea, and decided to go back to the river. It was very warm and, as I was climbing the slope of the dike, I remembered what Harumi said back in early May when we came up here; "*I smell summer coming.*" Now the summer was here without her.

As I always did, I took a deep breath when I stood on top of the dike and looked toward the bridge. The sun was setting and the sky over the bridge was orange red. I stood still and stared at the sky, and the color was glowing intensely. I knew what I had to do with my painting. I turned around and ran back home.

It was Saturday, July 31, the last day of school before summer vacation. There was no class, just the morning assembly and we were to receive report cards in the classroom. I brought the painting for Mr. Yoshida. The orange red sky transformed the painting into another world, and it became a much stronger work.

Mr. Yoshida called each and every student to the front and handed out the report cards.

"Have a wonderful summer," he said to the class after he gave out the last report card, and the class was dismissed.

Many of the kids screamed and ran out of the room. I waited until most of them were gone and then approached Mr. Yoshida.

"I painted this for you," I said. "The paint is still wet." I had to warn him as I was handing the painting to him.

Mr. Yoshida held the canvas in two hands and looked at the painting for a long time, his eyes were getting watery. He put the canvas on his desk, and without a word he turned to me and gave me a hug.

"Thank you," Mr. Yoshida whispered. "I'll see you at the graduation."

Saburo was waiting for me in the hallway. I walked down the staircase with him.

"When are you leaving?" I asked as we were coming out of the school building.

"Next week, Saturday or Sunday," he said. "I can't wait."

"You are lucky, you won't have to come back to this school," I said. "I'll be stuck here another seven months."

"The school wasn't bad for me though, not bad at all," he said and added, "Thanks to you."

We were at the gate. We shook hands, and said "Goodbye".

Jean Martinon

There was no summer break for my English lessons with Mr. Sasaki. After I said goodbye to Mr. Yoshida and Saburo, I came home and had to review what we had learned at the last session because we were going to have a lesson in the afternoon. It was progressing rapidly and we were almost finishing up the seventh grade textbook.

Takeo and I were told to bring our report cards. Mr. Sasaki looked at Takeo's card and congratulated him. He had a "5" which was equivalent to an A for his English. Takeo once told me that he had trouble with the subject in school, so his parents made an arrangement with Mr. Sasaki for private lessons. But now he was way ahead of the class. Mr. Sasaki glanced at my report card and did not say anything. I had five in all subjects but we did not have English in the elementary school.

After the lesson as we were walking out of Mr. Sasaki's house, Takeo told me that he was going to take charcoal drawing class in the nearby art studio during the summer. He asked me if I was interested in joining him. I told him that I did not think so. I had tried charcoal drawing once and hated it. Sitting around the plaster bust of figures like Venus, Caesar and Brutus and using a charcoal stick and a slice of bread as an eraser, I was supposed to draw the bust on the paper as accurately as possible. That was the drawing class Takeo was talking about. I was told by some people that without mastering this drawing technique I could not get into any art school. Mr. Okamoto, our art teacher in my school had mentioned this, and my father took me to the studio once and I tried. At the class every time I drew something, this college art student came around and erased what I had done and told me that charcoal drawing was not making art. I had to learn to be a machine and draw what I saw. He seemed to be more and more frustrated every time he came around and saw what I was doing because I was not following his instructions, and kept doing the drawing in my own way. When he tried to erase what I drew for the third time, I took the paper and tore it up, and told him I wanted to leave.

"You are hopeless, too young to be here to begin with," the guy said disgustedly. "Don't even think about applying to art school."

I thought if that was what it took to get into art school then I didn't need an art education. I knew I would never master such a technique and, by forcing myself, I could lose interest in art all together.

When I came home, Isao and Tomo were waiting for me, and my mother asked me to take them out somewhere so that she could clean the house.

The summer vacation was hell for our mother. She had to deal with five children all day, seven days a week in a small house. Quite often I had to take care of my two brothers during vacation. Mother gave me water in a canteen and some rice crackers for snack in a small backpack. I let Tomo carry it on his back and told Isao to get the insect net and cage from the shed in the garden.

As we were coming out to the street from the alley, we met Michiko and Hisako coming home from their piano lesson.

"Where are you going?" Michiko asked.

"We're going to the river," Tomo said excitedly. "We'll catch big dragonflies."

It had been a very hot and humid day but cooled down a bit, and on top of the dike, a gentle breeze from the river made me feel invigorated.

Between the river and the dike there was a wide grass field. We walked down through the knee-high grass to the middle of it, and I told Tomo and Isao to stay low and hide in the grass. Several big dragonflies were circling the field, flying low and catching small insects in their mouths. Those large dragonflies went fast, and they were not easy to catch with a net, but a few years of experience made me pretty good at it. One of them flew by me and I watched it go around and come back. I let it go around one more time and followed it with my eyes. When it came flying near me, I stuck the net out, and the dragonfly flew right into it.

"I got it!" I yelled.

"Wow, we caught a dragonfly," Isao and Tomo came running to me screaming. I let Isao take it out of the net and put it in the small cage.

It was a male dragonfly with a silver blue band on the front end of the tail next to the body. I wanted to catch a female which had a brown band because with a female we could catch male dragonflies easily and it would be more fun. I could use a female dragonfly to lure the males by tying it with a string and letting it fly circles around me. When a male dragonfly jumped on the female, I would bring them both down on the ground and then would catch the male by hand. They usually flew low between grasses laying eggs in water puddles. I walked around for a while looking for one but I could not find any. I gave up and looked up and saw a huge black one fly by me. Its wings and body were all black and the tail had yellow stripes on it. It was called Ogre Dragonfly and we did not see it often.

I watched it fly circles around the field and I positioned myself to catch it.

It flew right at me but it was too fast, and by the time I raised the net, it was long gone. I felt like the dragonfly was teasing me.

"Nobuo, come here!" Isao screamed, and I heard a dog barking.

"It's a doggy! Come and see," Tomo called out.

A small skinny dog was wagging a little tail vigorously and looking up at Tomo and Isao alternately. It had short light brown hair, but on one side of his body it seemed that the hair was stuck together with mud and it had dried hard.

"He must be hungry," Tomo said and took the backpack off his shoulder.

We all sat around the dog and I opened the backpack and took out a bag of rice crackers. The dog started to jump around us. I gave a piece of cracker to the dog and it started to eat with a loud crunching sound. I gave two crackers each to Tomo and Isao, and I kept one.

"He is eating, he is eating." As Tomo was screaming, the dog finished eating and was barking at me.

I was not going to give up my piece, but Tomo threw both of his crackers at the dog, and it jumped and caught one in the air. Isao gave one of his also.

"It's so dirty," I said and stood up because the dog started jumping on me.

"We should wash him in the river," said Isao.

"Good idea, wash him, wash him," Tomo chanted and started to run toward the river. Isao followed him and the dog ran after them.

I told Isao and Tomo to wait there and took my sneakers off and went into the water. I was wearing short pants. I called the dog but it did not come to me. I came out and held the dog in my arms and went back into the water. When the water was just about covering my ankle, the dog struggled and I dropped him in the water. The dog tried to run away in panic, so I had to dive onto it and hold. I was soaked and water was dripping from my shirt and pants. I noticed that Isao and Tomo were standing by me, also all wet. Three of us held the dog and scrubbed his body with our hands. We came out of the water, and the dog started to run around like crazy and Tomo and Isao were running after him. I took my shirt off and squeezed the water out and then put it back on. I told Tomo and Isao to do the same.

We had not realized that it was getting dark.

"Now, you are all cleaned up, so go home," I said to the dog, and the dog tilted his head to the right and looked at me as if trying to understand what I said.

"You go home, getting late," Isao said.

Tomo and Isao kept looking back but I hurried and walked up the slope and was on top of the dike. I saw the dog closely following my brothers wagging his little tail. We could not bring the dog home, I knew, because once I asked mother if we could have a dog, and she said that we could not afford another mouth to feed. Besides, father did not like dog at all.

When they caught up with me, I told my brothers that we could not bring the dog home and the reasons why. They were very sad, especially Tomo who was in tears. I held the dog in my arms and went back down the slope and left him in the middle of the field and ran back up the slope.

"Run!" As soon as I was on top of the dike, I yelled to my brothers.

We ran as fast as we could and stopped at the stone steps leading to the street, and looked back. I was shocked to find the dog coming right behind us. I sat on the step and wondered what to do. Tomo and Isao sat down beside me and put their hands on their cheeks, copying me. The dog too sat next to us and looked at me.

"Do you want to share your food with the doggy?" I asked.

"I will give my food to the doggy, yes," Tomo shouted.

"I don't mind," Isao said.

"You're going to be hungry, I'm warning you."

Our dinner table became like a war zone sometimes. Mother was a great cook, very creative, so whatever she prepared with limited ingredients tasted good, but we did not always have enough food for seven of us. We, children got into fights quite often over our share.

"But you said Daddy don't like doggy," Isao said.

"He doesn't have to go near him," I said, and decided to bring the dog home.

When we got home, mother was outside waiting for us. It was dark and we had no idea how late it was.

"What happened, Nobuo?" mother screamed. "We were so worried."

"We found a doggy," Tomo ran to mother and said. "Doggy followed us."

"Oh my goodness, you are all wet!" she said and looked at Isao. "You too, what happened?"

"We washed the doggy in the river," Tomo shouted." It was fun!"

Mother was very upset and yelling and screaming at me. Our dinner was ready on the table and I was very hungry, but she whisked us into the bathroom and we had to take a bath. We heard the dog barking as we came out of the bathtub. We dried ourselves and put our clothes on and ran to the front. The dog was barking at father in the entryway; it seemed like the dog tried to come into the house and father stopped him. Tomo went and held the dog.

"You cannot bring the dog in the house," father said to me.

"I know," I said and took the dog to the garden.

Tomo and Isao followed me looking worried.

"You wait here, I'll bring you some food," I said to the dog and he looked at me tilting his head to the right.

Michiko and Hisako came out and looked at the dog.

"What a miserable looking dog," said Michiko.

"He's a nice doggy," Tomo protested.

"What is his name?" Hisako asked.

"He doesn't have a name yet," I answered.

Finally we all sat down at the table and started to eat. I left half of the second bowl of rice, some miso soup and a little piece of broiled fish. Isao and Tomo were looking at me and doing the same. I went to the kitchen and brought a large bowl and put my rice in it.

"What are you doing?" asked mother.

"I am sharing my dinner with the dog," I said.

"Me too," Isao and Tomo said in unison.

Mother looked at our faces one by one and was speechless for a few seconds.

"You cannot use that bowl for the dog," she said. "Finish your dinner, I'll give you something for the dog."

Mother brought a ceramic bowl with a little chip on the edge. She put some rice and miso soup in it and cracked an egg over it and mixed it up and gave it to me. Tomo wanted to take it to the dog, so I let him.

"Where is he going to sleep?" Isao asked while we were watching him eat.

"He could sleep anywhere," I said. "Don't worry about it."

I waited till my brothers had fallen asleep. Michiko and Hisako were talking with mother in the next room. I had no idea what father was up to. I got out the futon and held my pillow under my arm and carefully went to the entryway, and opened the sliding door little by little just enough for me to get through. The dog was lying on the grass by the edge of the garden, but as soon as I came out, he sprung up and came to me wagging his little tail. I put my pillow under the bench and pushed him onto it. He lay down and stretched himself and curled up on my pillow. I came back into the house and went to sleep.

The next morning, as soon as we had finished breakfast, I asked mother to make some lunch for us. I wanted to go to the river and do some drawing. I was going to take my brothers and the dog with me. While I was putting things together, Tomo and Isao were playing with the dog in the garden. The floor to ceiling sliding window was wide open and Michiko and Hisako were sitting on the tatami floor and watching them. They were waiting for the broadcast of a music program on the radio.

The music started; it was Beethoven's Fifth Symphony.

"Nobuo, come and look," Hisako called out. "This dog likes Beethoven."

The dog was putting both paws on the bench looking into the room with his head tilted to the right. He seemed to be listening to the music. Hisako said the dog was running around but the moment the music started, he stopped and came over and posed like that.

"You should name him *Beethoven*," Michiko said.

"No, *Jean Martinon* is better," said Hisako, and told me that the music was the recording of the live performance by the NHK Symphony Orchestra conducted by Jean Martinon.

Jean Martinon was a French conductor/composer who had come to Japan as a guest conductor of the NHK Symphony Orchestra last summer and caused a sensation among music lovers. I liked the name, *Jean*. I thought it was the perfect name for the dog.

"Your name is *Jean, Jean Martinon*, okay?" I went to the dog and held his head with both hands and told him.

"Your name is *Jean*, okay?" Tomo repeated.

The dog responded to his new name right away.

I was supposed to meet with Takeo at the dike of the river. Mother asked me to take Isao, Tomo and the dog, *Jean Martinon* with me. I was very reluctant to do that because it was the first time I would paint side by side with Takeo, and I did not want to be disturbed by them. Mother pleaded with me and offered me to make a rolled-sushi lunch for everyone including Takeo and *Jean* if I took them. I could not refuse this offer.

Mother made Isao and Tomo wear thin short pants and rubber slippers, and told them they could go into the water if they took their shirts off. There may have existed but I never saw swimming trunks for boys. In those days in Japan, the boys usually wore a thin white cotton sash as swimwear, just as sumo wrestlers wore a thick silk sash for wrestling.

I carried the backpack which contained our lunch, a canister of water, some snacks, a towel, and the wooden oil paint case, and I made Isao carry the folded easel and Tomo a canvas.

Takeo was waiting on the dike. He was carrying a small backpack, a large wooden case, about twice as large as mine, strapped from his shoulder, a folded easel and, instead of canvas, a few painting boards tied together. He was very excited that I brought my brothers and the dog.

There were two strange looking big ships anchored in the middle of the river. I did not know what they were, but they looked very interesting. I mentioned them to Takeo and we decided to go by the river to have a close look. The ships were equipped with some kind of conveyer belts and they were making a loud rattling sound. Takeo said those ships were digging and taking gravel out of the riverbed to help prevent flooding and the gravel was used for construction. I decided to paint those ships but Takeo was not interested in the ships. Instead, he wanted to make oil sketches of the bathers. There were several people swimming in the river and some kids were splashing water on each other.

We each set up the easel and were ready to work. Tomo and Isao were already running in the field with *Jean* and heading to the water. I stopped them and took their shirts off and told them not to go too far into the water. There was no lifeguard, no swimming boundary and no warning sign.

While I was drawing two ships with a charcoal stick on the canvas, Takeo was working with oil paint directly on the board. He was using a small round brush and taking paint from the pallet and painting the bathers. I was mesmerized by his quick brush work. I really thought I was witnessing a genius in action. I could never paint like that, I thought. The way I painted was that I started with one corner and painted section by section.

By the time I painted the water surrounding the ships, Takeo was done with one painting which he called 'oil sketch'.

"Beautiful, Takeo," I commented.

"Thanks," He said. "Now I'm going to take a dip." He took his shirt and short pants off. He was wearing a white sash under the pants and he was ready to swim.

He ran to the river, dived, and with a breast stroke he swam quite a distance and came back. He was a good swimmer. I saw him talking to Isao and Tomo, and before I knew, he had carried Tomo on his back and started to swim. He went as far as the last time and came back. Then he took Isao on his back and did the same. The funny thing was *Jean* was swimming right next to him keeping the same distance all the way and back. I was totally impressed by both Takeo and *Jean*.

We had plenty of food for lunch. Takeo brought two large rice balls wrapped with seaweed, sliced roasted pork and fried sweet potatoes. We shared everything and had a real feast. *Jean*, of course, loved the roasted pork, but it was not his favorite. Surprisingly, he liked the dried squid best; he went crazy chewing strips of squid.

Takeo did not touch his paint brush again on that day. When we finished eating, Tomo and Isao asked him to give them rides in the water again. I told them not to bother him but Takeo took them to the river right away, and then he kept playing with Isao, Tomo and *Jean* nonstop. I saw him carrying Tomo on his shoulders, wrestling with both of them and running around with *Jean*. As I was watching him play with my brothers, I thought he would make a great big brother if he had younger siblings, and it made me think that I had to be better to my brothers.

I could not finish my painting and told Takeo that I would come back the next morning and try to finish it. He said that he would come by also but without any painting stuff. I thanked him for taking care of my brothers, and he replied that he hadn't had such fun in a long time.

Isao woke me up. He was telling me *Jean* was missing; he and Tomo had been looking for him and calling his name, but there was no sign of him. I got up and changed to day clothes and went out into the garden. Mother found my pillow under the bench yesterday, about a week after I had put it there, and was very upset. I told her that I didn't like the pillow and I didn't need one, that's why I gave it to *Jean*, but she did not want to hear it. I wondered if it had anything to do with this.

Tomo went to tell mother that *Jean* was missing. He reported to me that she said *Jean* might have gone for walk and should be back soon. Father was not there at the table when we were eating breakfast, so I asked mother where he was. She said he went to the temple for meditation and should be back for breakfast. I told mother that I would go and look for *Jean* with Isao and Tomo. She said we should come back by lunch time.

As we were going out the door, father came home.

"*Jean* is not here, we are going to look for him," Isao said to father. He looked at us and didn't say anything.

"We must find him," Tomo said.

"Where are you going to look?" father said in a low voice. "He must have gone home."

"What are you talking about?" I yelled. "This is his home."

Father didn't respond to that and went inside. We didn't know where to go except to the place where we found him, so we headed to the river.

We combed the field around the area where we found him calling his name. It was getting very hot. We walked along the river calling his name, and came back where we started and combed the area again. There was no sign of *Jean*. We sat by the water exhausted wondering what we should do.

"I am hungry," Tomo muttered.

"He may be home now," I said, and stood up.

"Yeah, he must be home!" Isao jumped up and said. Tomo got excited also.

We hurried home, but *Jean* wasn't there.

It started out as a very exciting summer vacation for me and my brothers because of *Jean*, but after a week it turned into the most depressing one because *Jean* was missing. Michiko and Hisako were concerned too. Although the degree of concern was different, it seemed that all of us had developed some kind of attachment to *Jean* in such a short time, except our father. Hisako played with him often, and I saw Michiko giving him fresh water because Tomo, Isao and I fed him regularly but quite often forgot to change the water in the can. Mother was seen giving him treats sometimes. When we brought *Jean* home, father declared that he did not like dogs and dogs did not like him.

Hisako told me that there was an article in the local section of the newspaper about a child who was bitten by a stray dog and died of rabies, and the town official decided to round up stray dogs in the area, especially along the Tama River. I thought it was possible that *Jean* ventured out to the street and was caught by the stray dog hunters.

We stopped going to the river and stayed around the house all day long driving mother crazy. When we met at the English lesson, Takeo asked me when we were going back to the river. I told him that since *Jean* disappeared we didn't feel like going there anymore. He was very disappointed. Father suggested that I go to see Tadashi before his leaving for Kyoto for training, but I just ignored him. I had a suspicion that my father had something to do with *Jean*'s disappearance. We missed *Jean* so much that Isao and Tomo cried sometimes.

It rained through the night and it was still raining in the morning. It was very hot but we couldn't even open the windows. Tomo, Isao and I were lying around doing nothing, I tried to read but could not concentrate. Michiko and Hisako were in the other room sitting at the table reading books.

I thought I heard a dog bark, but I wasn't sure. Tomo sprung up and ran to the front door. I heard him opening the glass sliding door. At the same, time I heard it loud and clear; *Jean* was barking. Isao and I ran and found Tomo holding *Jean*. The dog was soaked and all his paws were covered with mud.

"*Jean* came back!" Hisako screamed as she ran to the door. Michiko and mother followed.

"Tomo, you are getting wet, come inside," mother said. "To the bathroom!"

Tomo tried to stand up with *Jean* in his arms, but *Jean* was slipping down and Tomo could not get a hold of him. I took over and carried him to the bathroom. I put soap all over *Jean*'s body and, together with Isao and Tomo, we washed him sparkling clean. I brought him to the front room and sat down on the tatami floor. *Jean* adjusted his position on my legs and promptly fell asleep while Tomo and Isao were petting his head. It had taken him over ten days to come home. I wondered where he had been and what he had to go through to come back here.

Father looked really shocked to find *Jean* in the house when he came home. Tomo greeted him at the door and told him that *Jean* had come home. As he was coming into the room, before he could say anything, I said that *Jean* was clean and he was going to stay with me overnight. Father did not say a word.

The next morning, mother went out and came back with a small leather collar and a black leash made of fabric. *Jean* didn't like it when we put the collar on his neck, but he got used to it very quickly. We went out for a walk. Isao, Tomo and I took turns holding the leash. When we came home, we kept him in the garden with the leash tied to the big fig tree, but after dinner, we wiped *Jean*'s paws with a wet rag and brought him into the house. My brothers and I decided that we would never leave *Jean* outside overnight no matter what our father said.

The following Saturday, father came home a little early carrying some wood boards. He told us that he was going to build a house for *Jean*. We were surprised and delighted. We had never seen father make anything before, and it was really a great surprise to know that he was a good carpenter.

IN THE MUSEUM

I was looking at Harumi in the drawing, which was in a plain unfinished wood frame with glass. Somehow, she looked different from the image I had in my memory; the entire drawing looked different. The colors and composition were exactly as I remembered but the impression I got from the drawing, especially from the figure of Harumi was different. She was sitting on the rock by the water; her long black hair flowing down on her breast from her right shoulder and showing the left side of her face looking down on the water. Her face was in the shadow and you could not see her expression at all, but now I saw nothing but deep sadness in her face. I hadn't seen that when I was drawing the picture. Maybe it was just a reflection of my mind at the moment, but she looked as if she were gazing at her own death. 'What was she thinking when she sat on the rock posing for me?' I wondered. She looked stunningly beautiful. 'Was it the way she wanted me to remember her?'

"I like this picture," a pretty girl with a pink dress stopped in front of my drawing and said to the woman standing beside her. "Look at the girl's reflection in the water."

"Nice picture," said the woman, and they walked away.

Harumi promised to come with me to see the drawing if it were exhibited here when Mr. Okamoto decided to submit it for the competition. She lied. 'Did she know she was going to die?' I was asking myself the same question again, which, I knew, would never be answered.

The longer I looked at the drawing, the more disappointed I became. As an art work, it was not that good, I concluded. There were about a hundred works displayed in the room of the Tokyo Metropolitan Fine Arts Museum, selected from the works done by the sixth graders all over the country. Most of the works were watercolors. Some were done with oil pastels like my drawing, and there were several pencil drawings also. They were all good in many different ways, but one particular watercolor painting grabbed me. In the picture, a boy was sitting on the step of a rundown building next to a big garbage can holding a pigeon in his arms. The painting was not showing any feelings or emotion, rather it was just presenting a scene as is, cut-and-dry. I could not figure out why, but I was very much attracted to this painting. Aside from this, there was no work I could call extraordinary or striking, I thought. I would not remember any of them when I walked out of the room.

My father was patiently waiting for me in the middle of the room. He and I walked around the room twice studying every work on the walls carefully, and then I asked him to wait for me. I had to come back to my drawing alone and I was taking too much time staring at it.

"Your drawing looks good in there," he said as we were walking out of the building. "I am very proud of you."

"I wasn't as excited to see my work in the museum as I thought I would be," I said. That was the truth. When Mr. Okamoto told me that I had received the gold prize for my drawing, I was exhilarated; I couldn't wait to see my work in the museum.

"I guess I was more excited than you were, then," father said.

'If Harumi were here with me, things would have been different,' I thought.

The summer vacation passed very quickly after *Jean Martinon* came home. Takeo and I painted together by the Tama River twice, but he spent a lot more time playing with my brothers and *Jean* than painting. I went to see Tadashi at the temple once after he came back from his training session in Kyoto. He gave me a pretty intensive guitar lesson, and by the end of the day, I learned to sing *Molly Darling*, a song by Eddie Arnold in English with chords on the guitar. He told me that he liked my singing, and if my guitar improved, he might invite me to sing with his group.

The first day of the fall term, Wednesday, September 1, Mr. Okamoto came looking for me in the schoolyard in the morning before the assembly. He found me under the cherry trees, and informed me that my drawing was awarded the gold prize and it would be exhibited in the Tokyo Metropolitan Fine Arts Museum from September 5th for one week. He also said that the principal would hand me the certificate at the assembly, so when he called my name I should come up to the podium to receive it. I was very excited that I had received the gold prize and the drawing would be exhibited at the Museum, but I did not like to have it announced to the entire school, let alone having to go up to the podium to receive the certificate from the principal. Mr. Okamoto said that I had no choice.

We had a new female teacher; her name was Miss Ishino. She was very young and she had no prior experience in teaching at a public elementary school. I was curious to see how she was going to conduct the classes, so I was attentive all through the day. She was very good with keeping the students' attention; she was serious but sometimes very funny and always showing her passion and energy. I liked her.

On the second day, I resumed my routine; I placed a book on my lap and started to read. Miss Ishino was very quick to spot what I was doing.

"Nobuo-kun, you cannot read a book under the desk during class. You must pay attention to me," said Miss. Ishino as she was walking over to me, and took the book away. "If you want the book back, come and see me after lunch."

The book belonged to Michiko. I found it on the table that morning and I had borrowed it without asking her. It was titled *Shiosai*, 'The sound of the waves' by Yukio Mishima. Michiko had read and apparently loved it and kept talking about it, which made me curious.

As soon as I finished lunch, I went to see Miss Ishino in the teachers' room. If I did not retrieve the book, Michiko would be furious.

"You like books," she said. She was holding the book.

"Yes, I do," I replied.

"Do you like this kind of book?" she asked me.

"I don't know," I said. "No idea what kind of book it is, I haven't read it yet."

She looked surprised by the way I responded, so I changed the tone and explained that the book belonged to my eldest sister and I had borrowed it this morning.

"No wonder, I thought you were a little too young for the book," she was smiling.

"Is there any age restriction on the book?" I couldn't help saying. I hated the comment she made. 'Who's decision was it; too young to read this book?'

"No, no, I didn't mean that." She was obviously taken aback. "I was impressed by a sixth grader reading such a sophisticated book."

"The book was inspired by a Greek myth, my sister said," I said. I felt I had to say something.

"Oh really, I didn't know that. It's a beautiful story, I just read it too."

She gave me the book. "You must write a book report when you finish."

She took my pleasure away and tried to give me extra homework. I could not finish the book though. It was beautifully written but the story did not interest me.

One day, Miss Ishino made an announcement that the school was planning to put together the writing of sixth graders and compile a little book before graduation. She asked us to pick the most memorable or meaningful experience in our six years of school life, and write about it. It was long term homework, and we were supposed to submit it before the end of the fall term, but I wanted to do it right away.

At first I was going to write about Harumi's death, but I did not know where to start, and just thinking about it stirred up so much emotion that I realized I was not ready for it. I decided to write about Mr. Yoshida.

I titled my story 'Kamikaze Sensei', and wrote the story like this: My best friend died and I became desperate, lost interest in everything I used to love to do, and acted violently. One day, Kamikaze Sensei took me to the river and told me the story about two Kamikaze pilots; one of them was his close friend who played catch just before a suicide mission. The story taught me how precious *life* was, and in effect put me back on the right track. I ended the story with Mr. Yoshida giving me the catcher's mitt his friend had used.

It was only two pages long, but as I was writing, the events and their effect and my feelings and thoughts of the time became clearer. When I finished the story, somehow I felt much better; I also felt better about myself.

I gave it to Miss Ishino in the morning before the class, and she caught up with me in the hallway after dismissal.

"A very moving story, Nobuo-kun," she said staring at my face. "Thank you for sharing."

The drawing came back from the museum. Mr. Okamoto brought it to me in the classroom while we were eating lunch. It was in a cardboard case. He asked me if I could take it to the Fujiwara's house or if I wanted him to do it. He remembered that he had promised Harumi to return it to her when it came back. I said I would do it.

I came home and took the drawing out of the case and looked at it. It looked different again. This time, the whole scene looked warmer and more intimate. Harumi didn't look so sad either. I thought maybe I should keep it. I did not have a picture of Harumi and this was the only drawing she was in. Then I remembered that I still had Harumi's books. They were stashed away between my desk and the wall. I pulled them out for the first time since I had put them there that night. I picked up the shiny red leather bound notebook with the Snap-On belt. It was the notebook of Harumi's poetry. When I tried to open it that night, she had stopped me and said 'not now, sometime later.' I held it in my hands and wondered if I was ready to open it. I was not sure if I wanted to read what was written in the notebook. I was not sure if I wanted to know more about Harumi. Why had she given it to me? She had wanted me to read it sometime. Why did she want me to read it? She said that she just wanted me to keep these until she came home. She did not come home.

I was looking at the notebook in my hands for a long time, and finally I realized that I did not have the courage to open it; I was not yet strong enough. The notebook would be much more important to her parents than to me, I thought. The drawing would be too. I had given it to Harumi; it did not belong to me. I decided to return everything to Harumi's parents. I put the drawing back in the case, and the three books in the canvas shoulder bag.

"So nice to see you, Nobuo," Mrs. Fujiwara greeted me at the door. "Please come in."

I put the shoulder bag on the floor and the drawing on the table. Mrs. Fujiwara went out and came back with a glass of orange juice for me.

"How was your summer?" she sat next to me on the sofa and asked.

"It was great; I did a lot of painting," I said and took the drawing out from the case.

"Oh my, is this Harumi in the picture?" she screamed.

I had to explain the whole story to her: I did the drawing of Harumi by the river and had given it to her, but Mr. Okamoto sent it to the competition. It received the gold prize and it had been exhibited in the museum. It came back to the school, and Mr. Okamoto asked me to bring it to you.

"Why didn't you tell us? We would have loved to come and see it in the museum," she said as she held the drawing with both hands. "Are you sure we could have this?"

I just smiled and nodded.

"Harumi asked me to hold these until she came home, but..." I took out three books. "I wanted to return them to you."

She put the drawing down on the table, and I handed her the books one by one.

"This is Harumi's poetry notebook, this is Klee and this is the Andersen book."

"Thank you very much, but you don't need to return these." She tried to hand back the Klee book and Andersen book; A *Picture-Book Without Pictures*.

I thought about it for a second and decided to accept them.

"Will you come and see us more often?" Mrs. Fujiwara gave me a hug and whispered.

I did not respond to her, but I was saying to myself:

'I don't think so, Mrs. Fujiwara. I know I will never forget your daughter, but Harumi must remain as a beautiful memory of my past, and I must move on. As long as my heart keeps beating, I want to move ahead and face whatever comes my way. There may be a time when I feel I must visit my past, but not now. I will not come and see you again.'

EPILOGUE

Just about two months before the graduation, in the middle of January, Miss Ishino asked everybody in the class to exchange a one page note to each other. She said that since most of us had been together for six years, those notes from classmates could be nice mementos for the rest of our lives. I was not too thrilled about this project because I was wary of getting a lot of negative comments from classmates. I thought the majority of classmates hated me.

What a nice surprise it was to find out that many kids actually liked me. Some kids mentioned that I was fat, and one girl asked me what I was eating to maintain my size. Kenji and a few other kids gave me nasty notes, but most of them wrote rather nice comments about me. Some boys said that they wanted to be my friend but they didn't know how to approach me. One boy said that I was the most trustworthy kid in the class. I had no idea, but some girls were admiring me. Shizuko, the most popular girl in the class wrote that she wanted to say something negative about me and tried very hard, but couldn't find any; all she could think about me were wonderful things.

I realized that things could have been much different if I were more open-minded and had better perspective of the world around me.

Mr. Yoshida came to the graduation as he promised. He looked energized and happy. Kids were all so excited to see him. He gave me a picture of my painting hanging in his new apartment. He said that it had been such a pleasure to come home from work and see my painting on the wall. That was very nice of him.

I came to America after graduating high school and have been living in New York since 1963. I have been a struggling artist ever since. Over a half century later, I still have the books Harumi gave me; A Picture-Book without Pictures and the book of Klee's paintings. When my mother passed away and my brothers and I were sorting out her belongings, I found some of the notes my classmates gave me. I wondered why my mother had kept those, but Miss Ishino was right; they are indeed nice and amusing mementos.

Made in the USA
Middletown, DE
08 September 2019